Dear Reader,

Welcome to White Pine Island! Just a few miles off the coast of Georgia, this island is accessible only by boat, plane, and your imagination. Many residents call the island home year-round, but day visitors and tourists bring plenty of excitement with them. Like other resort islands, there are quaint shops, cool restaurants, and friendly bars. There are several resorts on the island, but the queen of them all is the elegant Grand Hotel on a bluff with an ocean view. Owned by the extensive, multi-generational Phillips family, the Grand Hotel offers elegant service, five course dinners, and plenty of romance.

In the first set of White Pine Island novellas, *Christmas at the Grand Hotel*, readers will meet siblings Ned and Ellen. They'll inherit the Grand Hotel someday, but for now they're busy working there—and finding love where they least expected it.

We hope you'll love the two novellas in *Christmas at the Grand Hotel* and return throughout 2017 for *Springtime at the Grand Hotel*, *Summer at the Grand Hotel*, and *Autumn at the Grand Hotel*. We'll look forward to seeing you!

Best wishes,
Amie Denman & May Williams

Christmas at the Grand Hotel

White Pine Island: Novella One
Ned & Bethany

by

May Williams

Copyright 2016 by May Williams
Christmas at the Grand Hotel
White Pine Island: Novella One
Ned & Bethany

All rights reserved. The unauthorized reproduction or distribution of this copyrighted work, in whole or part, by any electronic, mechanical, or other means, is illegal and forbidden.

This is a work of fiction. Characters, settings, names, and occurrences are a product of the author's imagination and bear no resemblance to any actual person, living or dead, places or settings, and/or occurrences. Any incidences of resemblance are purely coincidental.

Chapter One

Ned Phillips muttered a curse and deleted the third email this week from the Georgia Environmental Crusaders. He tossed his iPad onto the counter behind him, knocking over a pyramid of golf balls. Ned sucked in a breath as golf balls cascaded to the floor.

"Something wrong, boss?" Rob, his assistant, stuffed items into his backpack near the pro shop's door.

"Another threat from the Crusaders," Ned said, rapidly restacking the scattered balls. This so-called environmental group was under his skin. Their constant harassment pissed him off by challenging his work as manager of The Emerald, the golf course at White Pine Island's Grand Hotel.

"You sure it's okay that I take the whole weekend off?" Rob questioned. "We're so busy right now."

"You earned it," Ned said, "but you better hustle if you're going to make the last ferry."

"See you Monday. Thanks." With a quick wave, Rob cleared the door, jogging for the shuttle that would take him to the ferry dock in the village.

The kid deserved a break. Next week, they'd be up to their eyeballs in work. The holiday season brought a rush of golfers eager to indulge their passion. That was normal, no big deal, but Ned had another reason for wanting his course to be in perfect condition. And he sure as hell didn't have time for threats from some crazy environmental group.

He was one hundred percent compliant with the laws governing turf management, including the use of fertilizers and pesticides. And he was damn sick of being hassled about it from an agency that had no legal authority.

"Game of pool and a beer?" Grant called from the open door of the pro shop. "My fishing excursion finished early."

Ned glanced up at his cousin. The Phillips family, three generations strong, owned and operated the Grand Hotel. Each member had a specific area of responsibility. Ned's was the golf course while Grant managed outdoor programs and activities.

"Not today," Ned said. "I've got a four o'clock tee time still coming in."

Grant pointed behind him to the December sun hanging low over the distant mainland. "You know the sun's going to set soon, right?"

"Yeah, but it's Lou Hinkle."

"Ah," Grant said.

Ned's family hosted the Hinkles three times a year at the island resort. They spent lavishly but demanded constant attention, especially now with the upcoming wedding of Priscilla, their eldest daughter. Ned was thankful to be on the outskirts of that affair. All he was expected to do was play golf with Lou Hinkle, who was arriving early for a real estate conference.

"Maybe he'll get delayed. I could really do with a beer and some cheese fries." Grant snatched up three golf balls from a bucket and started juggling them.

"No luck. Ellen texted before taking off. She's flying him here now." Ned's sister headed the transportation department of White Pine Island's Grand Hotel. She brought guests to the island by ferry and plane, which seemed to feed her love of air and water.

Ned loved turf, the smell of a fresh cut green and fertilizer. Organic, of course. Environmentally friendly per Georgia's EPA policies. Putting the new guidelines into practice over the past year had increased his costs and cut his profit margin nearly in half. He was going to take some razzing at the end of the year's cost-evaluation meeting. The family members would probably award him the ugly brass cup, referred to as the Philly.

5

"Ellen should be a little less efficient sometimes," Grant suggested, deftly catching a ball and re-launching it.

"Don't tell her that," Ned said. "Maybe I can convince her to buy a new plane or boat before January first so she can win the Philly, or I'm a shoe-in." He shouldn't let it bother him, but as the eldest member of his generation working at the hotel, he felt extra pressure to succeed. He straightened a display of boxed golf balls, lining the edges perfectly.

"It's not so bad. I had it two years ago when I purchased enough stand up paddle boards and kayaks to make a bridge from here to the mainland," Grant said. "And even my fiscally responsible twin brother won the Philly when he put in that elaborate software system."

"Yeah, but Mike showed an almost immediate return on investment. I sure as hell won't." Ned's expenditures didn't work that way. He wasn't saving or making money on his recent improvements.

Grant stopped juggling as a vehicle's horn sounded. "Your tee time is here so I think I'll shove off. Join me later if you can." He slipped away as the van used to bring guests from the island's airport to the Grand Hotel stopped outside the pro shop.

"Hey, Yauncey," Ned greeted the driver as he opened the rear doors of the van. Yauncey had worked for the Grand, patiently and efficiently helping guests since before Ned's birth.

"I've got some folks eager to play a little golf," the old man said with a smile.

Folks?

"Hinkle's not alone?" Ned asked quietly, peering into the vehicle where two heads were visible in the van's second seat.

"Daughter," Yauncey replied softly as Ned rolled his eyes. The bride-to-be was a princess in training type. "Number two," Yauncey added with a wink.

Huh? The Hinkle's second daughter hated golf and hadn't even visited White Pine Island with her family for several years. The image of a dark-haired, lanky and gawky adolescent girl trudging insolently along behind her father on the golf course popped into Ned's head. Eventually, she'd refused to even step foot on a fairway.

She was going to golf? Today?

He shouldered Hinkle's golf bag and headed to greet father and daughter as they climbed from the van.

"Ned," Hinkle said after shaking his hand. "You remember my younger daughter Bethany, don't you?"

Ned turned to face the girl who'd made snide comments to him behind her father's back in the days when Ned caddied on the course.

Shit. Ned gulped down a gasp. This sophisticated beauty couldn't be the girl he remembered. This Bethany had straight, shiny dark brown hair, bright blue eyes, slim hips, and long legs clad in white pants. Who the hell…?

"Of…of course," he managed, stuttering. "Nice to see you again, Miss Hinkle."

She smiled at him and the super-model look dropped away. Now, she reminded him of the girl-next-door type who suddenly becomes a knockout.

"The place is just like I remember," she said, gazing up toward the bluff where the hotel sat. Round pillars supported the white four-story façade of the century-old building. The hotel faced out over the blue Atlantic Ocean toward the mainland, four miles distant.

"The beauty of the Grand Hotel is that it doesn't change," Ned said, not sure if her comment was praise or criticism.

"I guess," she said, quickly.

Make that criticism.

"Are you playing? I can get a set of ladies clubs," he offered, reminding himself that his role was to make sure the guest had a good experience.

"No, I'll just tag along behind Dad."

Just like old times, he thought. He'd be a glorified caddy, made uncomfortable by a girl—woman now—who hated what he loved most.

Golf was his passion, his true love. He played well enough to compete and did occasionally. He'd won tournaments, bringing home some nice cash prizes. Watching those events in progress sparked something else in him—he wanted to host a big tournament here on White Pine Island. A challenging and profitable prospect if he could land one. His first test was next week when tournament organizers would make a preliminary visit to The Emerald.

"Fine with me," he said, strapping her father's clubs to the back of a cart and wondering how he was going to manage her presence on the course. Ned always drove Mr. Hinkle, but that left Bethany facing backward and riding with the clubs. Not appropriate to the way guests were treated here. He kicked himself for putting the larger carts in the shed earlier. He didn't want to waste time by getting one out now.

Before he could figure out a solution, Bethany swung onto the cart's small rear-facing seat and crossed her long, slim legs. She caught him looking at her and raised one delicately-arched brow at him.

"Dad wants to get at least nine holes in before dark," she reminded him as if she golfed here every day and hadn't just materialized like a cicada emerging from its shell after a long hiatus.

"Right," he said awkwardly. "Can do." Which was even more awkward. How could she make him so uncomfortable in the one place he always felt in charge?

He drove to the tee box and started talking clubs, yardage, and swing technique with Mr. Hinkle. The usual golf course banter helped to center him if he kept the ugly-duckling-turned-swan out of his line of vision. For her part, she ignored him. He might as well have been invisible.

****

Bethany kept a keen eye on her father. His skin was still pale and he hadn't re-gained the weight he'd lost after the triple bypass surgery in September. He probably shouldn't be on the course at all, but he loved the game and his doctor had cleared him to play.

On the fourth hole, he made a long drive, his ball bouncing on the green far away.

"Nice one, sir," the golf pro complimented the shot.

Her father rubbed a fist across his chest as he handed his club to Ned. "Been a while—"

"Dad?" Bethany asked, rushing to her father's side and placing a hand on his shoulder.

"I'm fine for Christ's sake. I don't need a babysitter." He tried to shake her off, but she gripped both of his arms and forced him to make eye contact with her. She was nearly as tall as her father and wasn't backing down despite his gruff demeanor.

"I promised Mom," she said softly. "Maybe we should call it a day. Go relax and have a nice dinner. I'm sure Ned will get you a tee time tomorrow." She shot a pleading look at Ned, who nodded

"Not a problem," Ned said.

"I'll come with you then," she offered, trying to smile. "Maybe I'll even hit a couple balls."

"You hate golf courses," the older man muttered.

"No, I don't, and I like being out here with you. But not if you overdo it," Bethany said, real worry about her father's health making her queasy.

"I'm fine. I'm just out of practice," her father said, shaking her off. "Don't get old, Ned. All the women in your life try to boss you around."

She cut her eyes to Ned, daring him to agree with the masculine perspective. His expression remained polite, but neutral. The setting sun behind him emphasized his muscular build. He was taller than she remembered and certainly more attractive with his dark eyes and strong jaw.

A decade ago, she'd had a crush on him. Her crush ended abruptly the day she saw him kissing a busty lifeguard behind a hedge in the garden. At the time, she'd been a gangly girl with stringy hair, unable to compete with all that cleavage in a swimsuit. Bethany happily gave up golfing with her father and reluctantly gave up the hottie seventeen-year-old Ned.

Her father was making impatient clicking sounds. Before his illness, the sounds were a build up to a decision issued like an edict, but he'd slowed down. Now, he wanted her to decide what he should do—without it being obvious, of course.

"You poor thing," she teased, giving her father the out he wanted. "We care about you. I don't know how you stand it." Although she wasn't sure how much her sister Priscilla cared about him as long as he paid the bills and didn't screw up the fairytale wedding day she had planned.

"You win," her father said, tossing his hands in the air. "Take me up the hill to my suite, Ned."

"Yes, sir," Ned complied, quickly packing up the clubs.

Her father's theatrical capitulation didn't fool Bethany. He was genuinely exhausted after a day of meetings and travel. Tomorrow, he'd be ready for nine holes at least, which would give her the opportunity to photograph more of the golf course.

From her position on the golf cart's rear seat, she'd quietly snapped several photos of the greens and fairways and sent them off to her boss…her former boss. The playing surface at the Grand Hotel was flawless, too perfect for a course supposedly in compliance with the new environmental requirements.

Ned drove cautiously, slowing for corners and keeping to a sedate pace. The golf cart wound up the hill, past gardens to the inviting front porch of the hotel. The wicker furniture on the porch was grouped to create little intimate rooms where guests enjoyed pre-dinner cocktails. She studied the steps, the pillars, the potted plants. Everything was faultless. No chipped paint, no spent blooms, not even a pebble out of place.

"Like coming home to an old friend," her father commented when they'd stopped in front of the steps.

"We're glad to have you staying with us again," Ned said. "And we're looking forward to the wedding."

Sure you are, Bethany thought. The cost would add to the Grand's coffers nicely, not to mention some fabulous free press as various magazines published photos. Her sister's wedding plans had surpassed the category of *event* and moved onto *spectacle*. As a bridesmaid, Bethany was required to wear a puffy creation of pale pink, guaranteed to make her look like an overly tall cone of cotton candy.

"Lou, I didn't know you'd arrived," a rich baritone voice called from the porch. "Come on up and have a cocktail."

"Stephen, I thought you weren't coming until Tuesday," her father responded as he bounded up the steps, his exhaustion disappearing at the sight of his business associate and friend. Bethany would give him some time to talk with the other brokers but claim him in time to get a nap before the five-course dinner the Grand Hotel was famous for serving.

"I guess I'll check in," Bethany said, ignoring Ned's offered hand.

"Are you staying with your father?" he asked, still standing very near her. "I'm sure the luggage has been delivered to his suite by now."

"I have my own room. I'm getting too old to bunk with my parents and, frankly, I'll need some distance from the wedding hoopla when that gets into full swing." A separate room was an absolute splurge for her. Her parents insisted on paying for the week leading up to the wedding, but she was covering the cost of this first week herself.

Her parents were generous people, but she'd taken too much from them in the past year. Her job with the Crusaders hadn't paid enough to afford rent in Atlanta so she'd lived rent-free in a luxury apartment building owned by her parents. Her mother claimed she slept better knowing Bethany was in a secure building, but she was twenty-four now and it was past time to be independent.

Ned didn't comment about her room situation. His face remained neutral and pleasant. All the Phillips family members were well-trained hoteliers. Never making an out-of-line comment, never being disagreeable in public. His eyes, though, betrayed him. Their chocolate brown depths laughed, suggesting he understood what Priscilla's wedding would be like and probably dreading it as she did.

"I'll check with the front desk about your room," he said, gesturing her up the steps to the porch and following her through to the lobby.

Bethany halted just inside the massive front doors. "It's been redone," she murmured, gazing around. The lobby, always beautiful in her recollection, had all new furnishings and fabrics in shades of rich greens and burgundies. Floral prints intermixed with stripes and solids on the plush sofas and chairs.

"Last winter," Ned said. "How long has it been since you were here?"

"Four years. It's lovely. Comfortable and elegant at the same time." For the first time, she thought she might enjoy her extended vacation. Returning here suddenly felt like a kind of homecoming. She hadn't expected that. She'd come this week ahead of her mother and sister to keep an eye on her father's health—and for a job interview she hadn't mentioned to anyone.

"I'm glad you like it." Was that a hint of pride in his voice?

"I do. But what happened to the other furniture? I remember a blue velvet sofa at the far end, close to the windows. It was my favorite reading spot. It wasn't worn out certainly." She'd been looking forward to sitting there as an escape from the wedding drama, and she didn't like waste. Once an environmentalist, always an environmentalist.

"That couch is in my living room now. You'll have to stop by my cottage if you want to sit on it and read," he said and then quickly added. "I mean...it's one of the perks of being a family member. We get the castoffs." His ears turned pink and he looked away, his confident persona wavering.

"Where is your cottage?" she asked. What possessed her to increase his discomfort? He clearly hadn't meant his invitation *that* way. Why would he?

"Near the course." He pointed vaguely past the Grand Hotel's entryway. "It's just a little place that used to be a summer rental."

"Miss Hinkle," a petite strawberry blond woman greeted her and gave Ned a quick, searching glance. "I'm Cora, from the front desk."

"I remember you." Bethany smiled, picturing a ruffled apron on the woman. "You used to serve ice cream cones in the little shop downstairs. Is it still there?"

"Yes, but I've been promoted. No more scooping Neapolitan for me. I've checked you in and your bags are in your room. If you give me just a moment, I'll escort you up."

"I'll take Miss Hinkle," Ned volunteered. "Which room?"

Cora raised an eyebrow at Ned. "Four twenty-five. Your father is in four ten so you'll be just down the hall.

Thanks, Ned," Cora said, handing him a key, "and I hope you enjoy your stay, Miss Hinkle."

"Is Cora your sister?" Bethany asked after they stepped off the crowded elevator into the empty fourth floor corridor.

"Cousin. Ellen's my sister, the one who flew you over."

"Right, I remember now," she said as they reached her door. Ned unlocked the room, using the brass key, before handing the key to her. His fingertips trailed along her palm for a split second. Warm and inviting like his eyes. She swallowed. "No plastic keycards still?"

"Our guests prefer the traditional keys." He pushed the door open, revealing a room done in various shades of blue from cornflower to navy. Muted watercolor paintings of beaches and boats decorated the walls. The queen-sized bed had a white eyelet comforter and several decorative pillows in floral patterns. She could be very comfortable here for the next two weeks while she endured her sister's wedding and sorted out her future.

Her eyes swept the room, landing on the sheer curtains at the opposite end. "A veranda. I wasn't expecting that."

He walked ahead of her and pushed the French doors open. "These end rooms are smaller," he said. "But they have great views."

She placed her phone and purse on a table and followed him out onto the private veranda. A cushioned lounge chair, big enough for two, invited her to sit, but she walked past it to the railing and leaned out to admire the view. She could see the edge of the golf course, a sloping hill of pine trees, and a stretch of ocean.

"The roof near the beach is my cottage," he said from behind her.

A green roof poked out from among the trees. Why was he pointing it out to her when he'd been embarrassed to reference it in the lobby? Was he as aware of the strange tug between them as she was?

"I'll keep that in mind, in case I want to visit my favorite sofa or need some emergency golf lessons." She turned, leaning against the rail, to study him. He was tall and muscular, powerful-looking, and with a clean-shaven appeal. He'd taken his hat off in the lobby to reveal wavy, dark-blond hair.

"Right," he said. "I'll see you tomorrow on the course." But he didn't move until her phone rang, chirping and vibrating against the table near the room's door. "Let me grab that for you."

He brought the phone back, the screen lighting up with a distinct symbol, a southern live oak outline with the initials of the Georgia Environmental Crusaders forming its branches.

His eyes took in the screen and met hers. The hard look he gave her left no doubt. He recognized the symbol and wasn't pleased. Without a word, he handed her the phone and turned to leave.

"Ned," she called, not sure what she'd say if he stopped, but he didn't. The door clicked shut.

Damn.

She let the call go to voicemail. It was Paul, her former boss. He was probably thanking her for the pictures she'd sent earlier today and asking for more. She'd spent the last year working for the Crusaders, doing research, sending letters and emails when she uncovered infractions. It was good work, important work to preserve the ecological balance, but not what she wanted to dedicate her life to, especially now that some elements in the organization were turning to more radical and destructive methods.

She'd quit the Crusaders last week. A decision that would delight her real estate mogul parents since they'd never understood her desire to protect and preserve the environment. *Oh, they'd practically tap dance.* So she hadn't told them. Not until she had a new job doing what she wanted. Her stay on White Pine Island would hopefully bring her one step closer to that.

Bethany opened her suitcase, shaking the wrinkles from the royal blue cocktail dress she planned to wear to dinner. Would Ned be in the main dining room? She'd like another chance to talk with him, although she couldn't say why exactly. She sighed.

She dropped a pair of silver high-heeled sandals on the floor near the door and piled her hair on top of her head, playing with possible styles. If she did see Ned, making him a friend, not a foe, was her wiser option so she could learn more about the Grand Hotel's golf course and, perhaps, more about its attractive manager.

Chapter Two

"Beer and keep'em coming, Chuck," Ned said as he slid onto a stool at the local bar, a place tourists either didn't know about or avoided. *Good.* He didn't want to see any mainlanders at the moment.

"Glad you could make it." Grant broke off a conversation with one of the island's off-duty firefighters to plop down next to Ned. "You look like you need something fried, deep fried." Grant loved food, particularly the kind that took up residence in arteries. "Hey, Chuck?"

"Yeah?" Chuck, an islander, a few years younger than Ned, responded.

"What's the most disgustingly fried item you serve?" Grant asked.

Chuck thought for a second. "Fried mac and cheese served with fried pickles."

"With an order of French fries, I think. For Ned here."

Chuck glanced at Ned, waiting for him to nix the order.

"Why not?" Ned said. He was starving, having worked through lunch. He was in the final push of readying the course for the tournament officials' visit next week. All his plans were one-hundred percent on track unless some environmental Crusader derailed him.

"Coming up," Chuck walked the length of the bar and called the order to the kitchen.

"One of these days, you might have to take over food operations from your father," Ned commented. "You'll have to give up your love of fryers then."

"Nope, I'll leave the fancy stuff to our chef and come down here where Chuck will always fix me up. What's got you looking so glum? Was Hinkle a jackass? He's usually decent."

"He was fine, but he brought his daughter with him."

"Priscilla." Grant growled under his breath.

"Other sister. Bethany." Just saying her name churned his insides in a conflict that warred between attraction and anger.

"The younger daughter. Still dorky looking?"

"Not anymore," Ned said and took a gulp of beer.

"Interesting. Scale of one to ten?"

"Ten," Ned said without hesitation, thinking of her figure's slim curves.

"No way. So why are you drinking beer here? You should be eating in the dining room tonight. Maybe get a second look at her."

Ned shook his head. "You remember that environmental agency, the Crusaders, that keeps sending me emails and letters about compliance?"

"Yeah, why?"

"She works for them." A quick Google search on his phone had confirmed it. She was all over the Crusaders' Facebook page and her photo and bio showed up on the "about us" section of their website. She had a biology degree from Georgia Tech along with a minor in social justice.

"You sure?" Grant's face scrunched into a frown.

"Take a look." Ned tapped open Facebook on his phone and held it so his cousin could see.

"So you think she used her father's golf game to inspect the course?"

"I can't be sure," Ned said, "but I thought she was snapping pictures of the course."

Grant waved to the firefighter who was leaving. "You've got nothing to worry about. All those hoops you jumped through last spring put you above and beyond compliance."

All those hoops—implementing a new irrigation system designed to use effluent water, planting native trees and shrubs, stocking ponds with bug eating fish, installing bird and bat boxes as a natural mosquito repellant and a hundred other things.

"The Crusaders don't care about compliance. They care about headlines." Ned scrolled through his old text messages until he found a series of pictures. "I got this from the superintendent of a country club just outside Savannah. The course was in compliance, using approved pesticides. Look what those whackos did."

The pictures showed greens with deep divots carved in them, patches of grass dyed red in the shape of a skull and crossbones, and threats spelled out in white spray paint. Although the Crusaders had never been charged with the crime, the superintendent was damn sure they were the guilty party.

"They aren't kidding." Grant blew out a low whistle.

"The course was closed for over a month. I can't afford that on the Emerald, especially now with the tournament reps coming in next week. Any sign of trouble and we won't be hosting an event." Ned slammed his empty beer bottle on the bar. "I staked my three year financial projections on this."

He didn't have to explain to his cousin how much this meant to him and how many problems Bethany Hinkle could cause him.

"What's the matter?" Chuck came down the bar with a fresh bottle and huge plate of crispy brown food.

"Woman trouble," Grant said.

"You ain't fuckin' kidding." The bartender leaned heavily on the bar.

"How's Marian?"

"We're fighting about where to spend Christmas. I like an island Christmas, but she…shit." Chuck's marriage began as a one-night stand with a tourist that moved rapidly to a wedding and constant tension between the bar owner, a diehard islander, and Mainland Marian, who wanted to live where the ferry wasn't necessary transportation. "If this woman causing you trouble isn't from White Pine, stay the hell away from her."

"Thanks. That's my plan."

Chuck walked away to wait on another customer and watch the replays from the day's college football games.

"You sure that's the right plan?" Grant stole a fried pickle from his cousin's plate.

"What do you mean?"

"Think about it. If you got close to her...." Grant let it hang.

"I might know what she's up to," Ned concluded.

"Or she might feel bad about screwing you. Metaphorically speaking."

Ned ate for a few minutes while the idea sunk in. He was physically attracted to her. Hell, what man wouldn't be? Getting close might not be a hardship and it would only be for a couple weeks. Then, she would board a plane or boat off the island and out of his life.

"I've had worse ideas," Grant said, making Ned laugh. Lots worse, like the time they'd attempted repelling from the hotel's roof and crashed in the holly bushes. Or their indoor beach party that had the staff removing sand from the carpets for weeks. But this idea Ned considered, as Grant helped himself to more food.

Ned knocked his hand away after the second grab for French fries. "I may need to get dinner at the Grand if you keep eating mine."

"She probably looks hot dressed up."

Formal dress was a requirement in the Grand Hotel's dining room, dresses for women and dinner jackets and ties for men. Ned tried to picture Bethany in the kind of gown women usually wore. She'd be gorgeous. He imagined all eyes, at least the male ones, turning her way.

But there were several evenings to see her like that. Tonight, he might want her to worry about what *he* saw on her phone's screen.

"I think I'll wait for her to come to me," he said. "She's golfing with her dad in the morning." They'd decided on an early game before the conference got underway for the day. He wondered what Bethany would do while her father was in meetings.

"She might need some pointers on her swing."

"As the golf pro, I'm always happy to assist our guests," Ned said, and in the process, he could see what kind of game she was playing.

****

What was he up to? Bethany lined up her putt on the sixth hole's green, taking her time to sink this one. She was rusty and nervous, which made her current score almost double her father's. If Ned would stop looking at her with those dark eyes, she'd be less conscious of each stroke.

Not once had he mentioned what he saw on her phone yesterday. He'd been the kind professional all morning. He gave advice and helpful suggestions, but she'd botched every move.

"Straighten your elbows," he said softly, "and keep the movement small. Breathe in and—"

She hit the ball too hard and it bounced off the green into a water hazard.

Splash.

Biting down on the swear word on her lips, she strode over to the water in time to see her pink ball sink to the silty mud at the bottom. Dozens of little bluegill scattered at the unexpected intrusion. A large-mouth bass cruised over to see what the fuss was.

"One stroke penalty," her father called from his seat on the cart, as if she didn't know that. "You should listen to Ned. He knows what he's doing."

As if she hadn't figured *that* out in the past hour.

"Nice fish," she said, demoralized. "Some big ones, too." A few more bass, one as long as her arm, slid through the water.

"They help keep the insect population down without using pesticides."

Finally. That was his first reference to the course's compliance. And about fish, one of her favorite creatures and the heart of much of her studies.

She'd expected him to point out other features she'd observed as they'd traversed the Emerald. She'd noted several boxes, homes for bats and birds along the edges of the greens and tucked in the wooded areas. More insect control. The boxes were artfully designed to complement their surroundings because everything here was perfect.

Which irritated her for a reason she couldn't identify. What really annoyed her was that she'd been unable to take pictures of the immaculate playing surface because of his scrutinizing gaze.

Now, he was patiently waiting for her with a new ball to replace her lost one. He had to be angry with her from yesterday. She'd seen that in his face, but today, he was kindness itself. He dropped it in an advantageous spot, better than she deserved, and held a putter out to her.

"Thanks," she said, taking a glance at her father who had his head tipped back against the golf cart's seat and appeared to be dozing.

"Can I offer you some advice?"

"That's your job, isn't it?" she snapped, taking the club but instantly feeling guilty. "I'm sorry. I haven't played much in the past few years."

"You know how to play. Take your time and relax your shoulders," he said, placing his hand on her upper back. "You're too tense. The game is about enjoyment, being outside, spending time with people you love." He kept his voice low as he rubbed between her shoulder blades.

He stood close to her, close enough that she could have rested her head against his chest and given in to his gentle touch. She almost sighed, but covered the sound with a cough and jerked away.

"Okay, tell me exactly what I need to do here," she said.

With his advice, she sank her ball in the cup and moved on to a one under par on the seventh hole. *Oh, he was a master when it came to golf and golfers.* He joked with her father, giving him tips in a way the older man would appreciate. For her, he was an encouraging coach, who gave the impression that if she just tweaked this or that, all would be well.

She wanted to throttle him.

"Do you want to continue?" Ned asked after the ninth hole, where she'd made the par four rating. "I can drive your father up to the hotel and come back."

Her father had a meeting to attend as part of the conference, and she'd insisted that playing nine holes was enough while he was still recovering from heart surgery.

"Oh, I think I'll just take a walk. Plenty of time to golf in the next two weeks. The beach area looks really beautiful this morning," she said, starting off across the course toward the shore, eager to escape Ned's observation.

"You'll need to change your shoes," her father said. Two rules were never broken in her parents' household. Golf shoes were worn exclusively on the course and bourbon was served neat.

"Right. Can I get a ride back to the clubhouse?" She'd left her sneakers there. Planning to change quickly, she'd hoped for twenty minutes while Ned was occupied with her father to snap more pictures. The sooner she fulfilled her promise to Paul and the Georgia Environmental Crusaders, the better.

"Of course," Ned smiled at her.

At the clubhouse, she waved goodbye to her father, promising to meet him for a late lunch, stuffed her feet in her sneakers and took off as soon as the golf cart went around a bend. Earlier she'd spotted a maintenance building behind the clubhouse and pro shop. Getting in there would probably tell her a ton about the course's compliance.

Since it was Sunday morning and the course was busy, the other employees attended to players. No one paid any attention to her so she slipped between the buildings, yanking her phone from her pocket as she walked. She took some shots of the exterior but only to prove where she was. It was immaculate. Not a stray pile of fertilizer, not a random tee, heck, not even a mud puddle.

Someone, she guessed Ned, kept very tight control of this space, even in a place where guests didn't go.

The overhead garage doors were down so she tried the man door. Locked. Not surprising, considering what she'd observed about Ned's management. But the building had windows and, although they were fairly high up, she was tall. They were also immaculately clean, inside and out, she noted as she peered through the first one.

Mowers and other equipment were stored on this side of the building, but there was a partition down the center. What she wanted to see must be on the other side. She circled the building, again finding a row of windows. She cupped her hands around her face to block out the sun's glare and squinted as she gazed through the window. Tanks, pipes, a control center—this was the heart of the irrigation system. How many additives flowed through those pipes?

"I'll give you a tour if you like," Ned said from close behind her.

She whirled around. He stood not two feet away, his arms crossed over his chest, his face shaded by his hat.

"I was just...." Just what? Curious to know if The Emerald was polluting the environment and he was lying about compliance with Georgia's laws?

The shaking in her limbs and hollow feeling in her middle was why she'd worked in the Crusader's office, doing research and sending letters, and not been out sneaking around courses like some of her co-workers. This type of environmentalism wasn't for her.

"Always happy to show our system off," he said, taking a key ring from the pocket of his khaki shorts.

"If you're not too busy," she ventured, keeping her voice steady.

"My pleasure." He smiled and gestured toward the front of the building, waiting for her to walk ahead of him.

****

His grandfather's guiding voice pulsed in Ned's head. In 1956, his newlywed grandparents bought the Grand, restored every inch of the hotel and grounds, and built a reputation for world-class service. The rules pounded into Ned as a child about hospitality and service were what kept him from yelling, *get the hell away from my golf course,* at Bethany. That and he needed her on his side.

Instead of shouting profanities, he'd smiled and offered an unexpected service, just what he'd been trained to do.

He unlocked the door and stepped into the air conditioned building. The outside temperatures were mild today, but the blast of cool air helped calm his temper. A steady hum came from the control panel, and he glanced across the array of lights to make sure it was operating optimally. The iPad he used to control it sat on his desk at the pro shop, but he didn't need that to show his snooper what she came to see.

As usual her phone was in her hand. He wanted her to report his compliance to the laws to the Crusaders, but he wasn't giving them everything they wanted. So he lied.

"The company who designed this system for us asked that it not be photographed. They're in the process of patenting the technology and don't want it stolen. Sorry. I have to ask you to put your phone away."

"Sure," she said, quickly shoving her iPhone in her pocket. "Can you explain to me how this works?"

"Happy to. In order to have the least amount of impact on our environment, we went with an effluent system for irrigation. Are you familiar with that?" He'd bet the golf course's December profit that she was, but she shook her head, playing dumb.

"Fortunately, the island's wastewater treatment plant isn't far off our property. We built a pipeline from the plant to here to bring in water that couldn't be re-circulated for human consumption due to salt content, some heavy metals, bacteria and the like. We filter it again and use it in our irrigation system."

"So you're using water that would have been unusable. Very smart."

"Yep. It's a win-win for us and the island's administration. Disposing of that water was expensive because it can't just be pumped into the ocean."

"But doesn't it end up there anyway?" she asked "The contaminates have to go somewhere."

"Absolutely, but turf grass, the kind we use on the course, is an excellent natural filter. Our testing, done by an independent agency," he was careful to point out, "shows that the contaminates are gone by the time the water goes into the ocean as runoff or soaks back through to be groundwater."

"Fascinating." She gave him a pleasant smile. "How long have you had this system?"

"We installed it in February just ahead of when the new state laws took effect."

"It must have been costly."

"Yes, but necessary." He still lost sleep over the dollar amount involved in installing the system. The price of which was made even more expensive by their location on an island.

"Did you hire a technician to manage all this?"

"That's my job." He'd spent last January training with another course manager on Amelia Island in Florida to learn the system in an environment similar to White Pine. After attending Rutgers University Turf Management Program just out of high school, he understood water and grass. He just needed to know how to control the new equipment.

"But you're also out on the course. How do you keep up?"

Did she really care or was she trying to figure out what corners he cut? Probably the latter. She was still looking for the flaw, a nugget of information she could use against him.

"The Grand is a demanding mistress, but it's what my family does," he said simply, not giving her what she wanted.

"I'm sure. Family owned businesses usually are. My parents work a ridiculous amount of hours and it takes a toll, but they love it."

"Your father's health?" He took the opportunity to ask. Something was off with Lou Hinkle.

"By-pass surgery. Three months ago," she said and her face softened. "He's recovering well, but mom wants me to watch him this week."

"Nice that you could get an extra week off from your job."

A flicker crossed her expression. She didn't want to directly talk about her job. Then, maybe she shouldn't sneak around his golf course.

"I'm glad to know about your dad's surgery. I'll make sure he doesn't overdo on the course."

"Thanks. I appreciate that." She strolled around the room, peeking behind the pumps and tanks.

"Looking for something?" he asked, sticking his hands in his pockets as he leaned against a wall.

"Do you add chemicals to the water used for irrigation?"

"That's the beauty of the effluent system. No chemicals necessary. Only filters."

"But you use fertilizers and pesticides?"

"Some, but we spread them manually."

"Could I—?"

His phone buzzed loudly in his pocket and he pulled it free, checking the screen. Nothing was on the screen since he'd triggered the buzz himself. A trick he sometimes used to get away from garrulous guests or to extract himself from uncomfortable conversations, like this one.

He wanted Bethany to learn about his eco-friendly operation, but he wasn't giving up all the information like serving cake on a platter. She was going to have to work harder to find out what was stored in his chemical building.

"Sorry, I'm needed on the course," he said, looking apologetic.

"Of course." She walked to the door, giving the room's equipment one last glance. "Perhaps I'll see you later."

"I'm sure you will."

He waited until she strode off toward the hotel. She might double back, but without his guidance. He'd let her creep around on her own. In a few days, he'd find a way to reveal that he used the finest organic products money could buy.

How he'd love to be leaning over her shoulder when she reported her findings to the Crusaders.

Chapter Three

"Hey, Paul," Bethany spoke quietly into her phone as she walked up the hill through the gardens.

"Bethany? Christ. I know you're on island time, but it's not even eleven on a Sunday morning," Paul's voice, sleepy and irritated, reached her.

"Sorry, I've been up for hours and I've got a minute to myself and wanted to report in."

"Hang on," he said.

She heard rustling and a door close on his end.

"Okay, so what have you got?"

"Nothing. That's why I called." She sat down on a wrought-iron bench. Christmas roses bloomed all around her in a riot of colors. Oh, why couldn't she just enjoy being here?

"What do you mean nothing? I saw those pictures yesterday. No way is someone making a course in the South in December look like that without cheating."

"I just golfed with the course manager and saw the irrigation system. He's using one of the latest effluent processes. I think the course is clean. I really do."

"Did you see pesticides, fungicides, any of the cides? And what about fertilizers?"

"I didn't get that far, and I don't want to seem like I'm investigating him. I'm trying to be subtle." Okay so peering in windows wasn't subtle, but Paul didn't need to know she'd got caught doing that. Ned's reaction had been more than nice. He didn't have to show her the irrigation system. She wondered what made him take the time with her.

"Bethany, we talked about this. You can't be emotional about this hotel. It's a pretty place and important to your family, but you love the natural world more. What if this course manager guy is letting tons of chemicals run off into the Atlantic Ocean every year, killing fish and turtles and birds? What if that water circulates to the intake pumps of major cities and kids are drinking pesticides in their Kool-Aid?"

She sighed. Her former boss knew how to get her, which is how she'd come to agree to this last assignment with the Crusaders in the first place. "Listen, I promised to report what I found. But nothing is nothing."

"The chemicals, Bethany. You've got to see what's being used. If it's all good, then you're done and I put White Pine Island's Grand Hotel on the gold star list of approved courses." He wasn't joking about the list. Bethany had seen it, but only two courses state-wide had made the ledger so far.

"Okay, I'll see what I can do," she agreed. Golf courses usually spread chemicals early in the morning. Tomorrow, she'd take a walk an hour or so before sunrise and see what kind of activity was happening on The Emerald.

"Thanks. Hey, when's your interview at the turtle place?"

"Tuesday," she said, "and I'm using you as a reference. I hope you'll make glowing comments about my work ethic and knowledge."

The island housed a small turtle rescue center on its easternmost point. With the help of state and federal grants, the turtle center had recently expanded into a marine research station, where Bethany could study fish and aquatic mammals. A dream job for her. She'd been seeking a research opportunity since graduating from college. The position at the Crusaders, although interesting, was too loaded with conflict and controversy for her scientist's heart.

"I wouldn't be lying if I said you're the best employee I have and I'm sorry to lose you."

"Thanks, Paul."

"Nothing I can do to convince you to stay with me? I need cool heads like yours to combat some of my gung-ho staff."

Paul had fired the instigator of what could be called criminal trespassing when three Crusaders damaged a course in Savannah. She thought he should have turned the trio over to the authorities, but it wasn't her call. He'd made a convincing argument about the repercussions for the entire organization if the Crusaders were linked to unlawful activity. Since no one had gotten hurt, she'd said nothing, a decision she'd regretted but one that motivated her to look elsewhere for work in the environmental field.

"It's time for me to make a change. I'll be in touch." She clicked the end button and leaned against the bench's back. Stretching her legs out in front of her, she sunned herself for a moment. She closed her eyes and took in a deep breath of the fresh air.

The pines the island was named for were everywhere, but the Grand Hotel's gardeners had created lush landscapes with a variety of plants. The scent of flowers and a slight saltiness from the ocean blended into a delicious concoction.

"Miss Hinkle?" a soft voice said.

Bethany cracked opened her eyes. For a moment, she'd lapsed into a daydream in which Ned's hands were on her back again like they had been on the course and no one cared about golf course compliance.

"Hi," Bethany said, struggling to straighten her posture and dismiss her thoughts of the attractive golf course manager.

"I'm Cora. I talked with you yesterday at check in." Ned's cousin wore the dark green shirt-waist dress of the front desk staff.

"Yes, of course. Is my father...?" Bethany jumped to her feet.

Cora smiled reassuringly. "I just saw him in the lobby. He appeared to be fine."

"Good. He's been ill this fall." Bethany felt compelled to explain, although her father wouldn't like her saying it. This week it was her job to watch over him as much as he'd let her.

"Your mother called today to alert the staff, and we were sorry to hear that he'd been unwell."

"Thank you."

"I didn't mean to bother you, but I wanted to personally invite you to a program for some of our younger guests this afternoon. A group is kayaking or paddle boarding around the southern edge of the island. It begins at three."

Bethany hesitated. Her father would still be at the conference then, and she wasn't going to learn anything else about the golf course at that time of day. And it was just the kind of activity she loved.

"That sounds lovely," she said. "Do I need to register?"

"I can add your name to the list if you like. Be on the porch about ten minutes early and you can catch a ride to the beach."

****

Cora did her job, Ned noted from the driver's seat of a golf cart, when Bethany walked onto the hotel's porch in time to catch the shuttle to the shore. He could always count on his cousin to come through. Keeping Bethany occupied guaranteed she wasn't creeping around his golf course and it was a good opportunity for him to be friendly.

Despite his anger this morning at finding her in his maintenance area, he hadn't forgotten his master plan to play up a relationship between them. He didn't think she was the enemy exactly, but it wouldn't do any harm to keep her close, make her like him. He'd made progress on that earlier both on the course and afterwards.

Being around her wasn't a hardship. She was smart and beautiful, even with her hair hidden under a Georgia Tech ball cap as it was now. She wore a black sundress, but the strap of a red swimsuit peeked out.

"I think we have everyone," Grant said while standing on the porch steps, a clipboard in his hand. About thirty guests turned their attention to Ned's cousin. "We have plenty of kayaks or boards for everyone so take your pick. If you're new to paddling, Ned or I will give you a quick lesson before we get in the surf."

At the mention of his name, Bethany's eyes landed on Ned and she waved. This was going to be easy, maybe even fun, to have a little flirtation.

"Grab a seat on one of the carts and we'll get started." Grant pointed to the lineup of twelve passenger golf carts they usually used to take guests to the village or on tours around the island.

Ned watched Bethany making her way to his cart, but another guest intercepted her. Jordan Murray was a young attorney from Memphis here on the island for his parents' thirty-fifth wedding anniversary. Ned golfed with him yesterday morning and liked the guy until now. When Jordan put a possessive hand on Bethany's back to guide her along, Ned wanted to peel each of Murray's fingers away from her.

Bethany shot Ned a small, apologetic look and climbed into the cart driven by Grant. Murray leaned close to her, chatting away, but Ned felt a surge of satisfaction when she turned around enough to catch his eye. He gave her a nod.

At the beach, Ned hopped in a kayak and paddled into the ocean, making sure guests were safe after Grant launched them from the beach. Bethany picked a neon green paddle board and was upright as soon as she cleared the area where the waves hit the shore. Murray attempted to mimic her actions and did a dramatic and embarrassing somersault off the board.

"First time?" Grant called to the wet and bedraggled Murray. "Come back to the beach. I'm giving lessons in just a minute as soon as the experienced folks get started."

Ned wanted to high-five his cousin. Murray had no choice but to retreat while Bethany paddled her way directly toward Ned's position off shore. The red swimsuit turned out to be a bikini top with a little skirted bottom, which gave him plenty of well-toned muscle and golden skin to admire. Everything about her made his plan to get close to her simple.

"Is this part of your job as well?" She asked as she came alongside him.

"I help Grant with larger groups and whenever I can sneak away from the course." He grinned.

"I thought you loved golf."

"I do, but I can't resist the ocean. Look." He pointed between their boats as an Atlantic Stingray skimmed the sandy bottom.

"He's a beauty," she exclaimed and knelt on her board, peering more deeply into the water. A small school of Blue Runners darted past, shifting direction in the shadow of his kayak. "Wow. The water is so clear. How deep is it?"

"About fifteen feet here, but it drops off to two hundred just a little way out. Sometimes we see bull or tiger sharks cruising that area. Nervous?"

"Not at all." She stood back up on her board, easily keeping her balance despite the constant waves breaking over the nose.

He tore his eyes from her to scan the other guests who were making their way out toward him. Several looked to be experienced kayakers, who were competently managing the surf. He targeted a young woman struggling to establish a rhythm with her strokes.

"Don't go out too far on your own," he yelled to Bethany before paddling away to assist the fledgling kayaker. For several minutes, he worked with her and other guests, giving them tips and teaching techniques to make their experience better. Occasionally, he looked to where Bethany paddled. As she drifted farther from shore, she kept her gaze directed into the water.

"Rogue wave," Grant bellowed from the beach. He'd just launched the last of the guests and was paddling out himself, his legs dangling from the board surfer-style.

Ned turned to see the wave as it crested at least twelve feet high. It broke far enough off shore to only cause a rapid rise in water level and some bobbing for most of the group. Ned was scanning the surface checking on his newer paddlers when a neon green board shot past him, fin up, the ankle strap trailing behind it.

Bethany's board.

Shit.

She was in the water and probably caught in the big wave's hold-down. His eyes swept over the churning ocean. In shallow water, she'd be forced against the sandy bottom, which would be like slamming into a brick wall. The effect in deep water could be even worse as the wave would push her well under the surface.

No sign of her on the surface.

Putting every ounce of his muscle into his stroke, he paddled to where he'd last seen her. A series of feeder waves spun from the larger one made the water choppy, limiting his vision. He searched for her blue and gold hat. Nothing.

Twenty feet away from him, Grant scanned the waters as well while standing on his board. "There," he yelled and pointed ahead of him.

Ned power-stroked to the location. Her dark hair spread out across the water's surface as she coughed and wiped the salty-water from her eyes.

"Bethany." He reached into the water, half-pulling her into his kayak.

"Undertow took me right down," she said, gasping for air. "What a ride."

"Are you hurt?" His hands ran over her back and torso, any part of her he could touch.

"No," she said, blowing out a breath. "Just give me a minute to rest."

He pushed her heavy, wet hair back and cupped her face, his thumb stroking across her cheekbone. Her blue eyes shone so bright that his thoughts scattered.

Grant paddled over, towing her board behind him. His usually flippant cousin wore a serious expression. "Everything all right?"

"Yeah," she said. Ned's fingers dropped from her face as she turned her head toward Grant.

"You must be one hell of a swimmer," Grant commented, his usual cavalier grin returning.

"Country club butterfly champion, three years running. I'm good now," she said to Ned and dropped into the water. She swam to her board, tossing one long leg over it and hoisting herself aboard. When she got up, she waved to the other guests who were milling around nearby. "All better," she called. "Sorry to give you a scare."

"Scare, hell, I think I just lost a couple years off my life," Ned muttered, earning a pointed look from Grant. "What?"

"Nothing. Let's get moving."

Under Grant's direction, the group formed into a tighter bunch and paddled west toward the dropping sun, keeping the island on their right. The Grand Hotel's white surface glistened in the late day light and The Emerald earned its name. The golf course, in various shades of green, descended the slope, almost touching the blue Atlantic. When they neared the island's harbor and boat traffic picked up, Grant signaled for them to retrace their route.

"I'd forgotten how beautiful it was," Bethany said, paddling alongside Ned on the return trip as the Grand came into view. She'd drifted along, talking to various people during the excursion. Murray, now in a kayak, tried to stay near her, but he didn't have the skill as she weaved through the pack. Ned had watched from the back of the group, his usual position to assist stragglers. He'd kept an extra close eye on her red bikini.

"I'm glad you think so," he responded. Seeing the resort from the water always re-enforced to Ned how lucky he was. His grandparents, parents, aunt and uncle, and his fellow grandkids worked continuously to make the hotel a success. But he was lucky. Lucky to have been born a Phillips and have the care and stewardship of this place left to him, his siblings, and cousins.

"Will you always stay here?" she asked as though reading his thoughts.

"I have no reason to be anywhere else." He got off island, now and then, to play in a tournament, or travel with friends. When he returned to White Pine Island, he couldn't imagine coming home to anyplace else. "What about you? Are you happy where you're at?"

"I've lived in Atlanta for the past year or so. It's okay, but I'm ready for a change."

Did that mean she planned to leave the Crusaders? He wished he could just ask her. Maybe she wasn't his foe after all.

Chapter Four

Bethany swung her leg over the borrowed bicycle and knotted her long skirt with a rubber band to keep it from dragging against the chain. Business clothes probably weren't necessary for a preliminary interview at a marine research center, but she planned to impress so she'd put on a navy skirt with a creamy white silk blouse and wedge-heeled sandals.

She'd strapped her messenger's bag to the bike's rack. Inside, she had her credentials, resume, letters of reference, and a proposed research topic in the style requested by the center. She was ready.

Since she'd biked on the island as a kid, she had no concerns about getting lost. She headed down the Grand Hotel's long driveway to catch the Atlantic Loop Road that circled the island's outer ring. The research center was on the easternmost facing part of the island. She'd visited there frequently as a kid, especially when her family's vacation coincided with the summertime turtle hatching season.

After years of begging, her parents finally let her volunteer the summer she was fifteen. She'd held flashlights to guide the hatchlings to the ocean or patrolled the beach at dawn searching for new nests.

She coasted past a small white cottage with a green roof. Pulling off the road's edge for a second, she glanced up toward the hotel. Sure enough, she could see the verandas of the fourth floor. This had to be Ned's cottage. The tiny front porch had a swing and a braided rug.

She bent, pretending to adjust her skirt while spying on the house in case he was home. No other sign of habitation was visible, but Ned was excessively neat if the golf course was any indication of that. He wasn't going to have junk cars in the yard or even a *Golfer's Welcome* sign attached to his door.

39

Early yesterday morning, she'd taken a walk along the edge of the golf course. The only activity going on was the collection of balls from the driving range area. No chemical applications, not even mowing, and no Ned either.

She hadn't seen him since they'd parted on the beach after the paddling excursion. Some of the guests had stayed to enjoy refreshments. The iced drinks, canapés, and fruit kabobs tempted her and Ned. *Well, he tempted her, too.* She couldn't explain her attraction to him. Maybe it was the look on his face when he pulled her from the water or the stroke of his hand against her cheek. Either way, he was in her head and not because she was investigating his golf course.

She'd resisted staying with him after paddling, catching a ride with Yauncey back to the hotel instead. She wanted to make sure her father was resting before dinner. He wasn't. She'd found him socializing on the porch although he'd been drinking seltzer water with lime and not his usual bourbon neat. Later, they'd eaten a sumptuous meal in the dining room, but there was no sign of Ned last evening. She'd gone to sleep with a nagging disappointment.

He wasn't home now, she determined after studying the cottage, so she pressed down on the pedal, establishing a steady rhythm that would get her to her interview in plenty of time. Her route took her past another beach area and the remains of a Civil War fort before making the final curve to the turtle rescue center.

"Whoa," she exclaimed when the center came into view. In her teenage years, it had been a rambling one-story building, beaten down by weather. Now, it was a large two-story, gray clapboard structure with a landscaped entryway and a new sign. She biked over to park near the sign that read *White Pine Island Marine Research Center* in bold writing. In smaller lettering, another phrase appeared. *Built through the generous support of Edward and Catharine Phillips.* Ned's grandparents. Interesting.

"You must be Bethany? You *are* Bethany. I remember you from years ago," a familiar-looking gray-haired man said as he came from the building and greeted her. "I'm Dr. Chris Monroe, but the volunteers have always called me Doc Kit."

"Of course," Bethany said, remembering the active man who seemed to be working regardless of what time of day or night Bethany was at the center. "It's nice to see you again. I didn't realize...." She'd never imagined the same man would still be running the center.

"Neither did I until I saw you. I hadn't connected your name on the application with the skinny teenager who used to hang out with us. You grew up. Come in. I'll give you a tour of our new facility."

Bethany grabbed her bag from her bike and followed Dr. Monroe into the building.

"It's been wonderful having the new space," he said, descending to a lower level of the building as he spoke, where a bank of windows looked out over the Atlantic Ocean. "Now, we can focus on bigger projects."

"I see the Phillips Family is a benefactor." She hoped her comment would encourage him to speak about their role at the center.

"Absolutely. Two years ago, we were awarded a significant grant to study migratory patterns of certain fish and aquatic mammals, but we didn't have the space. I put the word out to the locals, hoping someone could help us. Ed and Cathy came through by giving us a large donation and orchestrating fund-raising for the rest of the money."

"How generous of them," she commented, assuming what was good for the island was good for their business as well.

"Their grandson Ned serves on our board now. I assumed someone from the older generation would take the spot, but he's the eldest in his generation on the island and, I suppose, the future of the business."

She smiled as she processed that information. Ned was on the board here, the place where she hoped to get a job. That complicated things. Their interaction so far was friendly, very friendly, but if she discovered something negative about his golf course, what would happen?

That question kept returning to her as she toured the new labs, all with state of the art equipment, tanks and artificial tidal pools, and the outdoor space dedicated to turtle protection and dolphin observation. The facility astonished her, far surpassing what she expected to find and making her nervous. Other researchers, many with more experience than she had, would be competing for the position she hoped to get.

And with Ned on the board…she fought down a wave of nerves.

She'd broken a cardinal rule of job searching by quitting her job before she had another. What if she failed to get hired here? She'd have to admit to her parents what she'd done, and they would instantly offer her a position in their real estate business. She wouldn't go hungry, but her heart and mind would starve. She wanted independence, a chance to really be self-sufficient.

More importantly, she wanted this job so she could make a difference for the environment. During her hour long interview, she presented exactly that case. Her skills, her hopes for her project, her dedication to the environment.

"One final question that I must ask all candidates." Dr. Monroe's amiable demeanor became more serious.

Here it comes. He's going to ask what sets me apart from other potential employees. She'd practiced this one after reading about common interview questions.

"If you get the position," Dr. Monroe said, "it means spending at least two years living on White Pine

Island. I bring this up because past researchers have found that to be a challenge. One even left part-way through his research, leaving the center to cover the expense of his grant. People don't like living without the conveniences of the mainland. I see you've been in Atlanta most recently. Could you be content with island life?"

"Oh, yes," she said quickly. "I've been on and off this island ever since I was a child."

"On and off," he repeated. "Staying here through the quieter months and having to fly or take the ferry to Oceanview when you need new shoes or to Christmas shop wears on people. And housing here isn't all like the Grand Hotel. Are you sure?"

"Yes, I'm sure that I would not tire of being here." She said it to assure him, but she felt the truth of her statement inside. She could be happy here in a little apartment or cottage. One with a green roof popped into her head. Not that she would be living there…with him…but it was the type of place that would suit her.

****

Ned's phone chirped when he stepped out of the shower. So far, he'd spent his one day off a week taking a run on the hilly roads in the island's center.

"Hey, Ellen," he answered. His sister's busy schedule and his meant that they rarely saw each other although they both worked for the resort and lived on hotel property.

"Hey, yourself. Cora's swamped at the desk with checkouts and asked me to call you. She says there's a guest with a flat tire on her bicycle on the loop road. Cora thought you'd want to go get *her*." Ellen put a year's worth of emphasis on the pronoun. "Who's the guest?"

"Where on the loop road?" he asked, letting his sister wonder for a minute.

"Near the fort. You have two seconds to tell me who we're talking about or I will tell mom you have a girlfriend."

"Bethany Hinkle," he admitted, not doubting at all who the damsel in distress was. If it were anyone else, Cora would have dispatched Yauncey or one of the bell hops.

"Nice. I did notice when I was flying her and her father over that she had…uh…matured in certain ways."

"You could say that." He wasn't going to admit what he was really thinking. Bethany was beautiful and sexy. Ellen would have a field day with that piece of information *and* tell their mother.

"So are you going to go help her?" she prodded.

"We're all about taking care of guests. You know that."

"In that case, I'll let Cora know the matter is resolved. Maybe you could bring Bethany down to Chuck's place some night."

"Not sure a local hang out is her thing, but I'll keep it in mind. See ya." He clicked off before she could ask any more questions about Bethany.

Fifteen minutes later, he spotted Bethany sitting in the shade of a live oak, her long legs stretched out in front of her. He pulled a Grand Hotel maintenance truck off the shoulder of the road.

"I hear you have a flat," he said, getting out of the vehicle.

"A sizzle and a pop." She imitated the sound, smiling up at him. "I considered walking back, but…" she pointed to her dressy sandals, "these shoes aren't made for walking. Thanks for coming."

"Not a problem," he said, giving her a hand as she stood up. He held on to her fingers longer than he needed to, studying her. Her clothes and the bag she carried weren't the usual kind that guests biked the island in. "Were you headed somewhere?"

"Coming back actually." She hesitated as if she wanted to say more and stopped herself. "I'm sorry to pull you away from the course."

"It's my day off," he said. She had to have noticed his jeans and t-shirt. He wasn't dressed for golf. Maybe she was trying to shift the conversation away from where she'd been. Was she meeting up with someone from the Crusaders? He dismissed that as unlikely. Why would they make the trek to the island and be so far from the ferry dock?

"Now, I'm really sorry," she said. "I bet those don't happen often."

"Once a week, most weeks," he said. His family expected all members to work hard and be available for guests, but days off were deemed equally important.

"Have I interrupted your plans for the day?"

"I didn't have any. You?" He'd meant to do some Christmas shopping, but spending the day with her suddenly sounded like a whole lot more fun than trying to decide on gifts. If he wanted to be logical, he could even rationalize the idea as part of his master plan to become friends with her to protect his course. When she stood this close to him, the dewy softness of her skin inches away, his desire to be with her had nothing to do with business.

"Not until dinner time," she answered, a slight hitch in her voice. Was she feeling what he was?

"Have you ever seen the island from a local's perspective?" It wasn't an invitation, just a query.

"No, but I'd like to if you'll show me."

She'd taken the direct approach, leaving him no room for doubt. He liked that about her. He loaded her bike in the truck's bed and held open the passenger-side door for her.

"I'll need to change." She pointed to her skirt as she slid onto the seat. "But I promise to be quick."

After the short drive, Bethany entered the Grand Hotel, giving Ned just enough time to trade in the truck for more appropriate transportation.

"Never been on a tandem before," she said as she rushed down the porch steps, wearing khaki shorts, a lightweight hoodie, and sneakers.

"Is this okay?" He'd assumed she'd be fine with the bicycle built for two. "I could get a golf cart."

"No, it's great. Better for the environment and I love biking," she said, already climbing onto the second seat. "Where to first?"

"The village for lunch. I'm starving. What do you like?"

"Anything as long as we can eat outside." The sunny weather with a slight breeze was nearly perfect. The humidity of the summer and early fall had dissipated, leaving cool nights and temperate days.

"I know a place," he said, putting the bike in motion down the winding drive of the hotel.

"I used to race down this hill when I was a kid," she called over his shoulder.

"Who'd you race against?"

"No one. Priscilla didn't run."

"I'm not surprised." Ned tried to imagine Priscilla, who became Miss Georgia Peach in her college years, doing anything that might make her break a sweat. "You two aren't much alike, are you?"

Bethany laughed. "You have no idea. Are you and Ellen alike?"

He thought about that for minute. They were probably more alike than different and as kids, his sister would have raced him down the drive and possibly beat him. She was the island's tomboy after all.

"More alike than different. I have an older sister and younger brother, too. They're both off island at the moment."

"Will they come home for Christmas?"

"I'm not sure about Kate." His sister's divorce was final a few months ago. The family wanted her to relocate to White Pine permanently, but she was still working through some problems. He hoped more than expected her to come. "Easton will be here around the middle of the month."

"Maybe I'll get to meet him," she said as they coasted into the edge of the village. Christmas decorations were going up on storefronts and lampposts all along the main street. The whole island was starting to feel the Christmas spirit. "This'll be my first island Christmas."

"You're not leaving after the wedding?" Her sister's wedding was on December fifteenth. He assumed the entire family would depart after that.

"Sure...I am, but I'll still get the chance to see the decorations. It's like there are fairies working at the hotel. Every morning, new decorations magically appear. Today, the dining room was completely transformed when breakfast opened. I couldn't believe it."

"The whole process takes about a week." When he was younger, Ned got pressed into service working from midnight until dawn. Nothing could be left half-done in an area for the guests to see. No boxes of decorations or ladders were allowed in sight. "We do the ballroom tree last, just before the island Christmas party."

"Is the entire island invited?"

"All the locals. We have it on a weekday night when the tourist population is low. It's the best event of the year." No one missed it. Most of the businesses in the village closed early. Last year, the Grand Hotel set luminaries along the road from the village and up the drive to the hotel. It was sort of like entering a fairy land.

"Are there many other Christmas parties at the Grand Hotel?" she asked.

"Dozens, some luncheons, some evening events, weddings like your sister's. My Uncle Charles says it's the busiest time of year for the dining and catering departments." He slowed the bike, coasting to a stop at a waterfront restaurant with outside tables. Nearby, the island ferry was backing out of its slip for the noon run to the mainland.

They hopped off the bike just as the ferry's horn blasted loud and long. Bethany drew in a rapid breath, but didn't shriek or jump. Ned shook his fist at his sister who waved to him from the pilot house as she maneuvered the boat away from the dock.

"Wow," Bethany said her hand on her chest. "My heart's beating double time now. I didn't expect that."

He rested his hands on her shoulders and rubbed down her arms. Her eyes met his and he'd never wanted to kiss someone so much. He leaned closer.

Chapter Five

"My sister likes to make noise," he whispered. "Are you okay?"

"Fine." Her fingers curled into the soft fabric of his t-shirt. She didn't remember putting her hands on his chest, but that's where they wanted to be. He had the look of a man just about to kiss her and she wasn't letting go. She parted her lips, expectant.

The beep of a golf cart's horn sounded behind them.

"For Christ's sake," Ned muttered. "You'd think an island would be more peaceful." He released her and waved to the man in the golf cart.

"A friend?" she asked, disappointed by the interruption. Would he have kissed her here in the busy village? She'd never know.

"Yeah, Ellen's best friend Pete. He's always where she is." A crease formed on Ned's brow.

"You don't like him?"

"He's a hell of a nice guy. I just wish…never mind. Let's eat and then I'll give you that local tour."

They ate fish and chips and sipped beers while talking about where they'd gone to school. She told him about her degree from Georgia Tech and crazy football weekends on campus.

"My father talks up your skills as a golfer," she said after finishing a story about her roommate's job as Buzz, the university's mascot. "You must have a certification of some kind, but I don't know what that is in the golfing world."

"I'm a PGA teaching pro. I completed that program right after high school."

"And came back here to live happily ever after." She pried a little more.

"Not exactly. I went to a two-year turf management program in New Jersey later."

"You were off the island for two whole years?" She just couldn't picture him anyplace else.

"No way. I couldn't do that," he grinned. "It was a couple of ten-week sessions in the classroom at Rutgers University and the rest was internships on the golf course of your choice."

"Let me guess. The Emerald for you."

"Yep. I'm an island boy through and through."

"So turf management school...." She raised an eyebrow, waiting for him to elaborate.

"Teaches you everything you need to know to run a golf course. What's a biology degree prepare you to do?"

She sighed. "Nothing if you ask my parents. Some people go to medical school, but that's not for me. Some work in labs, wearing white coats and booties on their shoes, but I can't do that either."

"So...?" He let the word dangle as he took a swig of beer.

"My focus was primarily on marine biology, and I'd like to work in that field someday," she said, and he gave her a funny look. She expected him to suggest the research center here, but he didn't. Did he not want her to stay on the island or did the look suggest something else? She couldn't quite read his expression.

"I guess that explains why you were busy watching the fish and missed that big wave on Sunday," he teased.

"I have a tendency to always be looking down in the water. It's gotten me into trouble more than once." Like the time she swam into the tendrils of a jellyfish, zapping herself, while watching crabs move along the bottom of the Chesapeake Bay.

"Seeing what's in front of you is a good thing sometimes," he observed.

"Yeah, I'm figuring that out," she said, tilting back in her chair and watching his face. He didn't miss her meaning as he met her gaze and grinned.

"Let's get out of here and go explore," he said.

A little thrill went through her. What did he mean by explore exactly? She was game for just about anything.

"Where to first?"

"You've probably done the loop around the island."

"Many times." The nine-mile loop was pretty much a daily ritual for her during her family's stays.

"Have you wandered around the center of the island much?"

"Nope. I tried, but I kept getting lost. My parents had to send a search party for me one time."

He laughed. "That happens to the locals even. I'll show you my favorite sight up on the hill and maybe later we'll make a stop at the secret beach."

"Now I'm curious." She leaned forward, lowering her voice. "A secret beach? Is there a hidden path to it? Did pirates once bury treasure there?"

"You'll see," he said, standing up and taking her hand as they walked to the bike. Their joined hands felt natural and good, not awkward like she'd experienced on other dates. She wasn't sure this was a date exactly, but she was sure enjoying his company.

They took a street out of the village that climbed toward the island's center. Ned turned down one road, then another, and finally onto a narrow gravel lane as they twisted and wound up.

"Are we there yet?" She peeked over his shoulder. "Wherever there is."

"Just ahead," he said as they passed through an open iron gate, half over-grown and decaying with age. The forest around them was thick, the pine trees moving slightly in the afternoon breeze. "Watch to the right."

She turned her head as they rounded a curve and gasped. An old plantation house in the low country style stood amongst the pines and live oaks. Dappled sunshine patterned the red brick of the two-story structure. A deep front porch ran the length of the house on the lower level with a balcony perched over it for the second floor. The home appeared abandoned with no curtains at the giant windows, but the glass was intact. Paint on the porch floor and trim peeled away, but no boards were missing.

"I had no idea this was here," she breathed. When they stopped, she didn't wait for him and rushed onto the porch to peer in the windows. "Does anyone live here?"

"Not for decades."

"But it looks strangely cared for. There must be a story."

He climbed onto the porch and leaned against a post, watching her. "Curious?"

"Yes."

"Willing to bargain?"

"What?" she asked. Was he going to ask her about her involvement with the Crusaders? She had no idea how to respond. She wouldn't lie to him, but telling the truth would ruin what was developing between them.

He pushed off the post, nearing her. "I want to kiss you, Bethany. A kiss and I'll tell you the story. I promise it's a good one."

Her lips tingled at his suggestion. "I've never made quite that kind of deal before. I'm intrigued."

"Is that a yes?" He stood only inches away now.

She reached a hand out, running her fingers along his jaw. He hadn't shaved today, which turned his all American boy image to sexy, dangerous man. "Yes," she whispered.

He wasted no time wrapping his arms around her and pulling her against him. He felt as good as he looked. Lean, hard muscle under warm skin. She ran her hands across his shoulders to the back of his neck and waited for him to start the kiss.

"I thought you were going to kiss me," she said after a few seconds.

"I am, but I want to get this right."

"Like setting up a shot? You don't want to miss your putt?"

"I never miss in the short game," he said as he closed in, his lips brushing her, nipping and teasing, until he deepened the kiss. Her knees went weak and she tightened her hold on him, giving in to the kiss and the moment.

"I like this bargain," she gasped, when the kiss finally ended. "How many other stories do you know?"

"If I run out of real ones," he said softly, kissing her temples, her cheeks, her forehead. "I'll start making them up."

****

He hoped like hell he appeared to be in control, but his mind and body were reeling. He had to step away from her or he would lay her down on the wooden porch floor and....

She clutched his shirt as he tried to put some distance between them. She'd touched him in the same way down at the dock, driving him crazy then and now.

"Bethany," he said but his words were silenced by her kiss. It was quick like the flash of a lightning bug, but with just as much mesmerizing power. Shit, he was in trouble.

"Tell me about this place," she said softly and let go of his shirt. "I think it must have some strong romantic powers."

He instantly missed the connection between them, but he needed the space to calm himself so he started the story. "A little romance and a lot of tragedy. We are in the South after all."

"True, but I always hope the romance outweighs the tragedy." She paced the porch, continuing to look in the windows as he sat on the porch rail and began the tale.

"Shawn Berkeley, the youngest son of a wealthy Georgia planter, built this house for his bride. He's said to have won the property, by which I mean the entire island, in a card game. Afterwards, he proposed to the girl from a neighboring plantation and brought her here in 1830 and began clearing land for cultivation."

"Romance, I'm satisfied so far." She paused, giving him a grin.

"Shawn and Elizabeth lived happily for a number of years, having five children."

"So far, so good. What happened to ruin it?"

"The hurricane season of 1848. The worst of the storms passed over the island in mid-September, causing significant damage."

"The house is still standing." She pointed out, tapping the brick with her finger.

"That wasn't the tragedy. As the storm struck, Shawn and his youngest daughter, who was four or five, were in an upstairs bedroom, closing the windows. A lightning bolt traveled into the house, killing both father and daughter. Elizabeth died a month later, supposedly of a broken heart. The house was abandoned as the grandparents claimed the remaining children and took them back to the mainland."

"That is tragic," she said, her face saddened. "Do you think the story is true?"

"It's documented in more than one place and on stormy nights it's said that in the flashes of lightning two silhouetted figures can be seen in the room where Shawn and his daughter died."

She shivered and rubbed her arms. "I don't think I like that part of the story."

"During the Civil War, the officers in charge of the fort on the island lived here, and then the place was abandoned again until 1904."

"What happened then?"

"The builder of the Grand Hotel came to the island. A few sturdy souls populated the harbor region, but John Barrow had a plan for a resort. He and his wife lived here during construction and for the few years they owned the Grand. Due to some bad investments, the Barrows lost the hotel in 1912 and the new owners built a home behind the hotel where my parents live now."

"When I was a kid, I always wondered where your family lived," she said. "I created this whole fantasy that there was a secret floor in the hotel, accessible only by the Phillips clan."

"Nothing that interesting, I'm afraid, although my parents' house is beautiful. I'm going to have to fight my sisters and brother for it one of these days."

She smiled at that. "What happened in the next hundred years?"

"Eventually, this place was forgotten and left to rot. In 1940, an investor purchased the house and a thousand acres surrounding it and started to pour money into restoration. When his son was killed in the D-Day invasion, he lost interest in everything and the project halted. Eventually, the state took control of it. Their intention was to knock the house down and use the acreage as a park."

"Knock it down?" she echoed, shock in her voice.

"It was the 1970s, everything was about urban renewal, not preserving the past. Fortunately, the state moves slowly and nothing happened. After several years, the house and land were put up for auction."

"Who bought it?"

"My grandparents."

"Ah." She smiled again. "How long ago was that?"

"About fifteen years. I was in the seventh grade." He'd been absolutely stoked, imagining that his family would move into the haunted house.

"Have you been inside?"

"Oh, yeah. My cousins and siblings all attempted to spend a night here."

"Did you make it?"

"Grant and I did, although it is pretty creepy late at night. The darkness here is extreme with these trees and no electricity."

"I'll bet." She studied the building. "You could turn it into a paranormal destination. People love that."

"It's been suggested at family meetings."

"You have formal meetings?" Her eyes widened.

"Every other month. All family members must attend because that's where major decisions are made."

She lingered near the plantation house's door.

"I'd take you in, but I didn't bring my key. Another day?" He could find the time to slip up here with her before she left the island.

"I'd love that," she said.

"How about some sunshine? The beach?"

"Secret beach. No regular beach will do after hearing this place's story."

"Worth the kiss?"

She turned to him, a flirtatious grin on her lips. "Definitely."

"Dinner after that?" He was a long way from being done with her company today so he pressed for more time with her.

"I'm supposed to meet up with my father," she said, hesitating. "But he has plenty of real estate friends to eat with. I could text him—or did you want to eat in the dining room?"

"I was thinking my place." So he could have her all to himself.

"Can you cook?"

"Not really, but the Grand's chef can. I'll swipe a bottle of wine from the cellar and take out from the kitchen, no dressing up required."

"I like to dress for dinner."

"You can if you like." He imagined her in a sexy dress and imagined taking her out of one just as quickly. "Be my guest."

"I think I will be."

Chapter Six

She sank onto the blue velvet sofa she remembered so well from the lobby. She'd read book after book sitting on its plush surface as her dad golfed and her mom and sister spent time shopping or in the spa.

In the little cottage's kitchen, Ned put desserts purloined from the Grand's kitchen on plates. They'd eaten entrees already and relaxed in his tasteful, but masculine living room. The blue sofa complemented a striped chair and the dark wood of the coffee table and book shelves.

"White chocolate mousse or cheesecake?" he called.

"I like both. You choose," she answered, resting her head against the soft cushions.

"We'll share," he said. They'd been sharing experiences and kisses all day. Their brief time on the secret beach culminated in a mind-blowing kiss and a whole lot of splashing in the water. She had no idea where this evening would end, but she enjoyed being in his company, his touch on her body, his lips on hers. Why not take advantage of the experience?

"No falling asleep," he said, coming into the room with their refilled wine glasses.

"I won't fall asleep. Yet," she said, taking a glass from him.

He flashed her a grin. As long as they didn't talk about the golf course, chemicals, or her work for the Crusaders, she could count today as the best romantic experience of her life. He was charming, intelligent, and handsome. What more could a girl want?

"I'll be back with dessert." He disappeared into the kitchen again.

"Don't they ask questions when you get dinner for two?" she asked.

"No questions. I did get a look from my uncle. He'll report to my parents and my mother will find a way to ask me about it."

"Sounds circuitous," she commented as he returned with two dessert plates.

"It is but easily circumvented." He'd divided the desserts between the plates, even drizzling raspberry syrup over them.

"I can tell you worked in the dining room."

"Mandatory. All Phillips must work in dining services and guest services for a year or two. I was an efficient busboy and prep cook. I even got promoted to waiter during one desperate evening."

"What happened?" She took a bite of white chocolate mousse and closed her eyes to savor the taste.

"Christmas break during my senior year in high school. Several of the kitchen staff went to the mainland to shop. The ferry broke down on the return trip, adrift for hours, until another boat could off-load the passengers. I survived the experience, but I have the upmost respect for our wait staff, who can memorize dozens of five course meal selections and never confuse who ordered what."

"I worked at the title department of my parents' real estate business one summer. So much paperwork to complete, organize, understand. That was not for me."

"You find what you're good at in life," he said.

He certainly had. His golf course was beautiful, consistently ranked as one of the best in the southeast, and squeaky clean as far as she could tell from an environmental perspective.

"I hope that's true." She should tell him about her interview this morning, but she feared jinxing the position by expressing her interest in it. That was silly and paranoid, but she wasn't ready, especially since he was on the center's board and might have an influence over who was hired.

They finished dessert and put their plates on the coffee table. "Now what?" he asked, giving her a scorching stare.

"We could play scrabble. I'm killer at that. I know a ton of scientific words."

"I like actions more than words."

"What kind of actions?"

In answer, he gently pushed her back on the sofa, covering her body with his. "Any kind that has me in contact with you," he whispered, kissing her throat.

"I like this game. Are there any rules?" She combed her fingers through his hair.

"Only if you want them." He lifted himself slightly so he could look in her eyes.

"No rules," she said, pulling his shirt from his waistband. She slipped her hands under the fabric and ran them over the skin of his chest and stomach.

****

Ned ignored Cora's raised eyebrow in the hotel's deserted lobby when he escorted Bethany to the elevators. After spending hours in his bed with Bethany, a discussion with his younger cousin didn't seem like the right thing to do.

He kissed Bethany goodnight and waited for the elevator doors to close. He didn't want her to go back to her room. He wanted to wake up with her in the morning, which was not his usual reaction to such situations. He'd tried to sort out his overwhelming desire for her as they'd walked up the long driveway from his place.

"Excuse me," Cora called as he passed her on his way to the doors. He gave her a nod. "Not so fast." She sprinted from behind the desk and caught up with him as he exited onto the porch. "I know you got dinner for two and I know that Bethany didn't eat with her father. Dinner time was about five hours ago."

"Don't you have something to do?"

"It's the nightshift, mid-week. Nothing is going to happen."

"I'm allowed to have a social life," he said, keeping his voice low. A crew was wrapping the hotel's pillars in white lights at the far end of the porch.

"Yes, but I should get a tiny detail because I'm the one who arranged for you to pick her up when her bike was broken." Cora poked him in the shoulder.

"We had dinner at my cottage."

"And?"

"Tiny detail given."

"I'm going to kick you in the shins like I did when we were kids." Cora, the youngest of the Phillips cousins, trailed around after him and Grant, continuously threatening them with bodily harm if they didn't include her. Sometimes, they let her tag along. At other times, they outran her.

"We had a *very* nice evening," he said, hoping she'd get his meaning.

"Did you have sex with her?" she whispered, gleeful shock on her face.

"Yes," he admitted, "now go back to the desk."

"My, my," she said. "This *is* going to be a special holiday season."

A few hours later, just as the eastern sky glowed with light, Ned strode across the golf course with his iPad and Rob, his assistant manager. They dodged sprinklers as they inspected various spots on the course. In less than a week, the tournament representatives would arrive and crawl over his course, inspecting every detail of his operation.

He had a checklist to make sure he and his crew stayed on track. His days would be packed with work, but he'd have his evenings free to spend with Bethany. She had commitments to her father, and her mother and sister would arrive soon as Priscilla's wedding day got closer. He'd move mountains to make sure he had time with Bethany after last night.

"Shit," Rob muttered. His attention focused on his cell phone.

"What?"

"Look at this." Rob handed over the phone. Images of a severely damaged golf course stopped Ned in his tracks.

"Where is this?"

"Just outside Valdosta. A buddy of mine works at the course. The Crusaders signed their handiwork." Sure enough, the Crusader's symbol was painted on the green in bright orange. "Bastards. Think they can get to us?"

"Yep." Ned yanked his cell phone out and hit the button to call his father. Ed Phillips would have been at work for at least an hour already and mornings were busy for the hotel's executive manager so Ned got right to his question. "Dad, what would it take to increase night time security on the course?"

They had two men who patrolled the resort during the night, but they could easily be someplace else when the Crusaders struck. He explained his worries to his father.

"Let me see what schedules I can move around," his dad said after listening for several minutes. "We might even be able to hire an off-duty officer from the local police force for the next week. I'll get back to you."

****

It was full daylight when Bethany woke to noise in the corridor. She glanced at her cell phone. Already ten in the morning. So much for checking out the fertilizer use on the golf course today. She could just ask Ned. He'd probably tell her everything she wanted to know and maybe even kiss her like he had last night. She fell back against the pillows with a sigh.

She'd had opportunity yesterday to put some questions to him, but couldn't. The day was too perfect to ruin. Now, how could she back-track without pushing him away? Her former job was the white elephant in the room although Ned didn't know it was former. She'd said she wanted a different kind of career, but she'd let the details remain fuzzy.

"Bethie, are you in there?" Her father knocked on her door, using his nickname for her.

"Just a second," she called, jumping out of bed and grabbing for a robe. When she opened the door, her father swept his eyes over the room behind her. "I'm alone." She clarified without mentioning that she'd spent time in someone else's bed before returning to hers. He stepped into her room, shutting the door and giving her a shrewd look.

"Is it Ned?" he asked, getting right to the issue. Her father had been a real estate expert for forty years and knew how to evaluate people and property.

"How did you know?" She tugged her robe closer around her, trying not to squirm.

"Easy enough deduction. I went to play golf yesterday afternoon and found it was his day off. You disappeared for the *entire* day and stood me up for dinner."

"I'm sorry about that," she said feeling guilty. She was supposed to be looking out for him this week, not hopping into bed with the hot golf pro.

"I didn't care." He chuckled. "Hell, I knew a hundred people at dinner."

"Did you eat well?" She tried to focus on his health that she'd neglected yesterday.

"It's the Grand. Everyone eats well. I got the salmon like a good heart patient." He strolled deeper into the room, glancing out the veranda windows. "You know I like Ned, don't you?"

How was she supposed to respond to that? Cautiously, she guessed. "I know you enjoy golfing with him."

"He's hard-working, a hell of a player, and a Phillips." The last was high praise in her father's mind. He'd been a loyal guest of the Phillips family for years and recommended the Grand Hotel to people constantly.

"It's nothing serious, Dad. We just…connected."

"Is that what it's called these days?"

"Dad," she whined. "What are you doing today? More meetings?" She was desperate to switch the conversation away from her personal life.

"The question," he grinned at her, "is what are *you* doing today? Your mother and Priscilla arrive in less than an hour. I thought you'd need some warning. You're going to want to fix your hair."

She glanced in the mirror. Oh, definitely. She needed a gallon of conditioner. Wild hair was the price for spending half the night with Ned, a price she'd gladly pay.

"I thought they weren't coming until tomorrow." Bethany knew it was still more than a week out from the wedding, and she was looking forward to her new plan for spending that week.

"Oh, they'll go back and forth to the mainland a couple times I'm sure, but they're coming. I'll be in meetings. Should I expect to see you at dinner?"

"Of course," she said. Returning to Ned's cottage for another meal and more time in his bed sounded like more fun, but she was here for her family this week.

"You can invite Ned to join us," he said on his way to the door.

"I'll think about it." For about two seconds. She refused to put Ned at the mercy of her mother and Priscilla.

After her father left, she showered, straightened her hair, and put on some makeup. She thought about dressing in a way that would appease her mother and sister, then discarded it and went for a casual dress, bare legs, and sandals.

An hour later when she greeted her family, her mother and Priscilla were dressed exactly as she'd imagined. Skirted suits, pantyhose, and pumps. Her sister wore pale blue which complemented her golden blond hair. Other than blue eyes, the sisters had little in common in appearance. Priscilla was a tad shorter, much curvier, and in a constant battle to stay slender. Her light-colored hair was a combination of wonky genetics and regular visits to the best colorist in Savannah.

"We're meeting with the wedding planner this afternoon," Priscilla declared after they'd greeted each other. "My maid of honor can't get away for a few more days so you'll have to stand in for her."

"I'm happy to," Bethany responded to what was really a command, not a request. Her friends wondered why she wasn't the maid of honor at her sister's wedding, but she was happy to be relegated to fourth bridesmaid status. Less pressure, less hairspray, less gushing.

"Your father tells me that you've been keeping busy," her mother said.

Bethany waited for further comment, but her mother seemed done. She guessed her father hadn't said anything about Ned. "Dad's been a good patient. He's eating well, drinking little, and getting exercise. Just like the doctor advised."

"He looks marvelous, better than he has in months. Thank you for missing work to watch him. With the wedding, I just had too much." Her mother had been working double time at the office to make up for her father's absence during his illness, and she was helping Priscilla with the multitude of decisions and details that accompanied a society wedding.

Bethany smiled, accepting her mother's thanks. After the wedding, she'd be forced to admit that she wasn't missing work. She was unemployed at the moment. The thought made her a little queasy. If she didn't get the research center job...she couldn't think of that now.

"When's the meeting?" she asked instead.

"Over lunch. We should go," Priscilla checked her silver Cartier watch, a gift from her neurologist fiancée, and swept toward the suite's door.

A flagstone terrace, extending out one end of the Grand Hotel, was a favorite spot of female guests. During the day, the staff set tables and chairs to serve a light lunch and afternoon tea. On nice evenings, a string quartet or jazz musician played soft music while cocktails were consumed.

Audrey Phillips and her daughter Samantha waited for them under a brightly colored umbrella in a private nook. Bethany had paid little attention to the wedding plans, but enough to know that Ned's aunt and cousin were the planners of events at the Grand.

The talk immediately turned to table settings and decorations. Samantha displayed several photographs of possible settings, which were scrutinized with the utmost care.

"I like this," Priscilla pointed to the dishes in one pictures after long minutes of scrutiny, "with this." She indicated the glassware arrangement in another.

"That's fine," Samantha took notes on an iPad.

"But I can't have roses on the tables," Priscilla declared. "I know we talked about red roses for the holiday theme, but no. Everyone has roses. I want red and pink orchids and not those easy-grow kind that are so popular now. I want true orchids."

"And for the white?" Samantha's fingers hovered over the iPad.

"Peonies. I saw the most beautiful white peonies at a wedding last spring."

"We'll have to consult with our florist on the mainland. Peonies are out of season in December and not a flower typically grown in hot houses," Audrey Phillips, a polished looking woman in her fifties, commented.

"Please check. If you can't get peonies," Bethany's mother said, "I'm sure something else will do."

"I don't want things *to do*, mother. It's my wedding." A pout crossed Priscilla's lips. This was going to be reminiscent of the time when she hadn't gotten the five thousand dollar pageant gown. Their father insisted that the three thousand dollar dress was just as lovely. Priscilla sulked for days and blamed her father for her second place finish in Miss Teen Georgia.

"Let's check before we worry too much about the flower arrangements. We left a few details of the menu open at our last meeting, but today those must be finalized," Samantha said firmly and read the proposed menu from her screen.

When the discussion of soup, chilled potato-leek or chilled tomato-watermelon gazpacho, lasted for ten minutes, Bethany's attention wandered. She gazed off toward the golf course down the hill. Players traveled from hole to hole, but she sought one particular person. She'd just spotted him when her sister huffed at her.

"You're supposed to be helping," Priscilla chastised her.

"Are we still on soup?" Bethany asked when she realized all eyes turned to her.

"Mother," Priscilla said impatiently, in the same tone she'd used since they were children to get what she wanted.

Bethany guessed they'd moved on from soup, and she'd missed it while searching for Ned on The Emerald.

Bethany bit back the unpleasant words in her mouth and forced a smile, reminding herself that her sister would only marry once, hopefully, and she should be nice. Throughout the rest of the meeting she made comments and suggestions, and her eyes only wandered twice to the green paradise of the golf course.

Chapter Seven

Ned straightened his tie as he crossed the Grand Hotel's porch. He'd worked until well after dark, readying the course. He was dog-tired and should have grabbed a beer from his fridge and crawled into bed. Except for one problem, he couldn't get Bethany out of his mind.

Instead of crashing and getting the sleep he hadn't gotten last night, he was headed to the ballroom for after dinner dancing. He might, he reasoned, make a complete ass of himself. Maybe she didn't want to see him. Maybe last night meant nothing to her.

They'd had no contact today. He'd dismissed that fear easily enough earlier. He didn't have her number and she didn't have his, which was ridiculous in the twenty-first century.

Cora worked the front desk again and smirked at him. Christ, didn't his younger cousin ever get a day off? His Uncle Charles raised a dark eyebrow at him from the entrance to the dining room.

He ignored his relatives, walking through the lobby to the open doors of the ballroom. The Grand Hotel's band was already playing, *In the Mood*, which was the siren call used to gather guests to the nightly dance. He paused at the entryway, scanning the room for Bethany's dark hair.

Blondes, redheads, silver haired women—he skipped past all of them until he spotted her. She faced away from him in a gold dress with a low scooping back. Her shiny hair was twisted up in a fancy style.

One problem. She was dancing with Murray, the lawyer from the paddling adventure. His hand was on the bare skin of her lower back and he held her close as the song shifted to *Sentimental Journey*.

Hell, no.

Ned crossed the floor, zeroing in on the couple. The training his family instilled in him since infancy screamed he shouldn't cut in. Guests should never feel a moment's displeasure if possible.

Ned had no personal beef with Murray, but the other man wasn't finishing this dance with Bethany. She was his.

He tapped Murray's shoulder. "May I?" he said politely, but it wasn't a question as he deftly took her away from the young lawyer.

"That was smoothly done," she said, giving him a secretive smile as he steered them to the far corner of the dance floor. "Poor guy seemed a little bewildered."

"Do you mind?" He let his hand slide across the smooth skin of her back.

"Not at all." She was a little breathless. "I've been thinking about you all day."

"That's exactly what I wanted to hear." The fatigue in his muscles disappeared with her words.

"Ahem," she said, tilting her head and pursing her lips.

"What?" Did she want him to kiss her here?

"You are supposed to reciprocate my words. Have you been thinking about me?"

"Yes." He tightened his arms around her as they swayed with the music. "I've been thinking about how much fun I had with you yesterday and the incredible way you made me feel last night," he whispered close to her ear. "It's been a distraction."

"Oh," she said, her face blushing. "I've had trouble focusing today as well."

"Your parents," he had time to say in warning before the other couple was beside them.

"Ned," Bethany's father said. "I'd like to play a round in the morning. Have you got time?"

"Absolutely, sir." He nodded to Mrs. Hinkle, unaware until now that she'd even arrived at the resort.

"You two have fun," Mr. Hinkle said as he and his wife slid away.

"I didn't know what to expect there." Ned let out a breath. "He must not suspect that we...."

"Oh, he does," she said quickly.

"But..." he argued. Mr. Hinkle and Bethany were close. Ned had watched how she'd fussed over him on the course and his protectiveness of her. What did it mean that the older man didn't object to Ned being with his daughter?

"I'm twenty-four years old," she reminded him. "I think my dad understands that I'm an adult and capable of making my own choices."

He accepted that for the moment, but anticipated an interrogation on the course tomorrow. "What about your mom? When did she get here?"

"She and Priscilla arrived this morning, unexpectedly. Wedding plans had to be finalized." She smirked.

"Is that what you did today?" He tried to picture her discussing floral arrangements and selecting chair decorations alongside her sister.

"Yes, it's not my thing, but I'm trying to be a good bridesmaid until her friends get here to take over."

"What would you have done if your mom and Priscilla hadn't come?" He wanted to hear her talk about anything as long as there was music and she was in his arms.

"That depends. In this imaginary day, would you have been with me?"

It thrilled him to know she wanted to spend time with him. "Answer both ways."

"My plan for the day was to take a bike ride and maybe explore at the plantation house more. There's something almost magnetic about the place. I can't explain it."

That's how he'd always felt about the plantation house. As a teenager, he'd spent hours wandering in the rooms and traipsing over the property. When he offered to show her the island, it was the first place he wanted her to see. He couldn't explain that either.

"If you were with me," she continued, "I'd probably have wanted to do the same thing except we'd have gone inside and you'd have shown me the romance and tragedy up close."

"I'll take you back there as soon as I can," he promised, pressing his forehead to hers, "but I'm swamped at the course. Is there anything else we'd have done?"

"We'd have ended the day in either your cottage or my room." Her voice was low and sexy. "As a matter of fact, that's still in my plan for the day."

"What if I hadn't put on a suit and come up here?" he asked, so happy that he'd made the right decision this evening.

She dismissed his question with a tiny shake of her head. "I would have found my way to you."

Heat rose through his body. "Let's get out of here. Take a walk. It's a beautiful night and I want to be alone with you."

****

As they slipped from the ballroom, Bethany noticed her sister dancing with one of their parents' business associates. Priscilla caught her eye, a look of surprise on her perfectly made up face when she noticed Bethany's companion. Priscilla gave Ned a critical glare.

"Your sister doesn't like me," Ned said, putting an arm around Bethany's waist.

"It's not that." Her sister didn't like anyone who would detract from her spotlight, especially this close to the wedding. Priscilla played center stage on a regular day. Bethany didn't want to think about the narcissistic behavior in the next week.

"You're more beautiful than she is," he said in a low voice as they crossed the lobby.

"It's not a competition." Bethany learned long ago not to vie for attention against her sister.

"And smarter and sexier," he kept going until they reached the porch, "and nicer." She laughed at that. It was the one category where she could guarantee a victory over Priscilla.

"Oh," she gasped. Thousands of tiny white lights decorated the Grand Hotel's iconic porch. "I see the fairies were working again."

"Last night."

"Gorgeous and romantic," she murmured, walking the length of the porch with him. Candles burned in holiday-dressed lanterns on the porch's many tables. Red and white velvet covered cushions and pillows replaced the usual stripes and floral patterns.

"Your family goes all out for the season."

"The entire island does. Just wait until it gets closer to Christmas."

"I'm not sure...." She stopped herself from saying that she might not be here. She'd heard nothing from Dr. Monroe at the marine research center. If she didn't have that job, she couldn't stay, not if she wanted to work in her field and be independent of her family.

About Ned, she had no idea what to hope for. She met his eyes, the unspoken question between them. Was this a casual fling or something more?

He took her face in his hands and kissed her, which didn't provide an answer, but erased the tension. "The best view of the hotel is from the gardens," he said, breaking the silence.

"Are you trying to lure me into the dark?" she teased, getting back to the romantic fun of a few minutes ago.

"Yes, and then we'll have to make a decision."

"About?" A flash of concern went through her. "My cottage or your room?"

At one in the morning, they strolled back to the hotel, hand-in-hand. As it turned out, the decision was obvious. They'd wandered in the gardens and admired the hotel from different vantage points, leaving them near his cottage. With one kiss on her back's bare skin, he'd set a fire that had them racing for his bedroom.

The tempo slowed when he lifted her dress over her head and she unbuttoned his shirt. She gripped the muscles of his chest with her fingertips as he kissed her and slowly backed her to his bed. She'd only had two lovers prior to Ned, but neither of them could compare. He made her feel beautiful and adored as he took his time pleasing her.

She sighed as they walked, and he tightened his fingers around hers.

"I'm keeping you up past your bedtime. What time do you get to the course?"

"Around six," he said.

"Won't you be exhausted?"

"Maybe, but it's worth it."

"You work hard. No life of privilege for the Phillips kids." She liked that about him. He was so dedicated to his responsibilities.

"Our livelihood depends on the success of the hotel. We were raised to understand that."

"Did you ever want to do anything else?" She'd been unwilling to follow her family into the real estate business. For him, it seemed so natural.

"No," he was thoughtful for a moment. "I play in a few tournaments every year, which require me to be away."

"PGA tournaments?"

"No, but competitive events with prize money on the line."

"Do you win?"

"More than I lose."

"Did you ever want to go pro?" She'd wondered about this since she'd frequently heard her father praise Ned's skills as a golfer. He could probably do it if he dedicated the time.

"And be off the island for months at a time? No way. My goal is to host—"

A flashlight's beam swept across them and Bethany blinked against the intrusion of light.

"Identify yourselves, please," a firm but polite voice demanded.

"It's Ned Phillips."

"Sorry, Ned." The flashlight clicked off and an officer approached. He shook hands with Ned, tipping his head to Bethany.

"How's it going?" Ned asked the young police officer.

"Quiet. I haven't seen anyone for over an hour. Not sure it's necessary for me to be here, but I don't mind the overtime."

"I appreciate having you around. It takes a load of worry off me."

"No problem. Have a good night," the officer called and headed in the direction of the course.

"Is something wrong?" She touched Ned's arm but he stiffened.

For several seconds, he didn't answer. Finally, he said, "probably not. I'm just being cautious. A lot of people come to the island for the holidays and some of them don't behave well. That's all."

Without taking her hand again, he started walking toward the hotel. There was definitely something behind his worries. Was it the Crusaders? Had they vandalized another course? She hadn't heard about it if they had, but she also hadn't checked in with anyone from the environmental group's office or social media.

In silence, they walked the rest of the way to the lobby's elevators. He kissed her cheek, a formal gesture and out of place with their intimacy earlier. She tried to smile at him as the elevator doors closed, but his expression was flat, almost sorrowful.

If they were going to continue seeing each other, she had to tell him about her work, her previous work, with the Crusaders. Every time she considered saying something, she stopped herself. She rationalized her silence based on his behavior. He'd had opportunity to ask her questions about her former job and hadn't. Did he fear what that conversation would do to them as much as she did?

Chapter Eight

Two mornings later, Ned woke in Bethany's room. She still slept, curled into his side, and he wanted to stay like this forever. He should have left during the night. Hell, he should have stayed away from her, but he was completely unable to do either of those things.

Every day he promised himself he wouldn't seek her out in the evening. He should put some distance between them. He'd started this relationship to watch her and protect his course, and he still didn't know what role her employment with the Crusaders played in her visit here. She could be spying on the course, even playing him to get information.

Still, when he finished work and went to his cottage, he never hesitated. He put on his dress clothes and sought her out. They danced, had a drink in the Grand's little speakeasy, strolled the grounds, talked for hours, and made love.

If she was spying on him, she was a master spy. As far as he knew, she hadn't even been to the golf course in days. If she was playing him...well...he didn't want to think about it. He couldn't imagine her being so devious. He looked at her sleeping face, her soft breath on his chest, and stroked her dark hair. She was the most beautiful woman he'd ever been with. And with each day closer to her sister's wedding, he felt the real possibility of losing her.

No matter what was going on with the Crusaders, after the wedding, she'd return to the mainland. For the first time in his life, he questioned living on an island.

"You stayed the night," she said, her voice thick with sleep. She wrapped her arms around him and rested her cheek on his chest.

"It's almost dawn. I've got to go soon."

She growled, making him laugh. "When do you get another day off?"

"Not until Thursday."

"What day is it?"

"Monday." The tournament representatives would arrive early tomorrow and stay just one day. He had twelve hours to impress them and show off The Emerald. As long as nothing happened, he was on track to be ready for their inspection.

"Right. Another day of wedding stuff," she groaned. "Who knew there were so many decisions to be made?"

"Does getting married have to be that complicated?"

"I hope not. I'd think a stretch of beach at sunset with your family and friends around would do it. But what do I know? Priscilla informed me that I was being naïve yesterday because I didn't think it mattered that all the bridesmaids had the same color nail polish. Apparently, we all have to go to the spa together to achieve the required uniformity."

"When does that occur?"

"The morning of the wedding."

"It'll be over soon," he said, but he didn't find any comfort in that.

"I want that," she said, tilting her head so she could see his face, "and don't at the same time."

She didn't have to explain her meaning. They both understood she'd be leaving and what they had might be lost. He didn't want to think about that. Instead, he rolled them over, pinned her to the bed and made love to her, savoring every second they had together.

It was almost light outside when he left her room and headed for the back stairs that only staff used. If he was lucky, he could get out of the hotel without encountering any family members.

He didn't make it. His mother spotted him from her office when he exited the staircase on the hotel's lowest level.

"Ned," she barked. "I need to see you." His mother was usually a kind person, but when he'd gotten in trouble as a kid, she was the disciplinarian. Her bite could be as bad as her bark.

"Good morning, mom," he said, entering her office, where she managed all aspects of housekeeping for the Grand.

"Close the door," she said. "Coffee?" A carafe sat on her desk to feed her caffeine addiction.

"No thanks." He waited for her to start the conversation although he didn't doubt what its content would be.

"Are you leaving a guest's room?" She poured coffee into a Grand Hotel mug.

"Yes." His cell phone vibrated in his pocket. Probably Rob wondering why the hell he wasn't at the course yet. He ignored it. Nothing infuriated his mother like excessive cell phone checking.

"Is that guest Bethany Hinkle?"

"You know it is," he said in a way that got him a sharp stare.

"And you know we don't run that kind of hotel. *We* do not engage in indiscretions with guests."

"Mom, it's not an indiscretion."

"What is it then? You've known each other for little more than a week."

"We've known each other for years. I remember her as a kid." Another text message came in.

"You aren't selling this to me as a we've-loved-each-other-since-we-were-teenagers sort of thing?"

Love. The word shocked him. He was having fun with Bethany. He cared for her, but love? That was momentous, that was the perfect wedding on the beach she'd described to him just an hour ago. He swallowed, imagining the sand, the water, and Bethany as a bride. As his bride.

He couldn't let his thoughts go there. Too much stood between them, but his heart hammered in his chest.

"Look, mom, I'm twenty-seven," he said, fighting to keep his face neutral, "who I sleep with is my business."

"Not when you're sleeping with a guest. What do her parents think? Has her father said anything to you?"

"Not directly, but he hasn't objected either." His phone vibrated with a third message in two minutes. A creeping fear went through him, unrelated to this contentious conversation with his mother.

"I've always liked Bethany, but the Hinkles are valued guests. You need to consider carefully what you are doing."

"She'll be gone in a week. Princess Priscilla will get married and...." He didn't finish his sentence, simply raised his hands in the air.

"This *is* serious between you and Bethany." Her steely expression turned sympathetic.

"I don't know," he admitted. "It's...something."

"Oh, honey, I'm sorry," his mother's usual kindness returned.

"I've got to get to work." He pulled his phone from his pocket and scrolled through the messages. "Shit," he said and sprinted from the room.

"How the hell did this happen?" Ned skidded to a halt next to the building that housed his irrigation system, the lifeblood of any golf course.

His crew, Grant, and most of the Grand's maintenance guys were already there evaluating the damage. The outside of the building was covered in orange and green spray paint with the Crusaders' symbol clearly scrawled on the door.

"Bastards." Ned punched his fist against the symbol.

"Outside is just graffiti shit," Grant said. "Easily fixed. But they got in."

"Fucking bastards." Ned sucked in a breath. "How bad?"

"I don't know a damn thing about the system. Calm down and take a look," Grant said. "We killed the power to the building because there's water everywhere."

His cousin was right. He needed to get himself under control, evaluate the damage, and figure out how to deal with it.

"I shut off the valve as soon as I saw it," Rob explained as they entered the building. Water, a couple of inches deep covered the floor, slowly heading for the drain. A pipe connecting two of the tanks was smashed. The system wouldn't operate without that pipe, but it could be replaced quickly.

Ned swung his gaze to the control panel mounted on the interior wall. The lights that usually flashed were dark. Someone had smashed in the left side of the unit with a heavy object. He strode across the room and forced the damaged panel open to study the interior. Maybe he could replace some parts and salvage it. At least enough to get through the next few days.

The tournament representatives would expect a working sprinkler system. Hell, they'd expect a course with security.

"Where was the cop we hired when this happened?" he demanded while he examined the control panel's components.

"There was a fire about five this morning in the hut on the back nine." The hut, tucked among a strand of pine trees, was a place to take refuge during lightning storms when players were too far from the club house or pro shop.

"They created a diversion? Are you fucking kidding me?" Ned forced himself to take a deep breath.

"The cop put that out, but didn't see or hear anything else," Rob explained.

"I called the police chief," Grant said. "There looks to be a fingerprint in the spray paint. He's sending someone out to gather that. He's also checking ferry passengers this morning, looking for people who have spray paint on their fingers or anything suspicious. We know they have to get back to the mainland somehow."

It was a good idea, but private boats and even planes left the island constantly.

"All right," Ned said, snapping into action. "Let's get the water out of here so we can turn the power back on. I'll need a paint crew to fix the damage on the outside of the building and someone to see what shape the hut is in."

"You got it, Ned." Rob and the head of maintenance ducked out the door.

"Call Ellen and get her on standby," Ned continued. "As soon as I figure out how much damage there is, she's going to have to fly to the mainland for parts."

"Can you buy those at a hardware store?" Grant pointed to the high-tech components.

"No, she'll have to go to Augusta where the company that built this has its production center. Tell her to gas up her plane, and I don't give a shit who needs a flight to the mainland. I get priority."

Ned yanked off his suit jacket and hung it over a pipe.

"Isn't that what you were wearing last night?" His cousin nodded to his jacket.

"Yeah. Why? You aren't going to give me a hard time about that, too?"

"Didn't you tell me that you caught Bethany snooping around and showed her this equipment?" Grant asked.

In one stride, Ned reached his cousin. He grabbed Grant by the collar and pushed him against the wall. "What are you suggesting? You think she had something to do with this? That's bullshit because I was with her all night."

Grant pried Ned's fingers away and shoved him back, straightening his shirt before speaking. "I'm not saying she did it personally, but you know who she works for. She could have fed them information so they'd know to hit you here." He gestured to the equipment all around them. "Where it hurts the most."

Ned turned his back, staring blindly at the smashed control panel. He didn't want to believe that Bethany betrayed him, but it made sense. She'd gotten information from him and used it to stick a knife in his back.

Except....

"I didn't tell her about the tournament rep's visit." He felt a moment of hope. She couldn't know that striking today would inflict twice the damage.

Grant snorted at that. "It's not a secret. Most of the Grand's staff probably knows. Just because you didn't tell her directly doesn't mean shit."

Ned was on the verge of telling his cousin to go to hell, but Grant was right. Bethany could be, probably was, behind this.

Chapter Nine

Bethany wandered out of the ballroom that evening. She'd danced for a while, but her heart wasn't in it without Ned. He'd usually joined her by now. Maybe she should change and walk to his cottage. He could have fallen asleep. The man worked long hours, and she'd been keeping him up at night. She suppressed a grin, remembering how she'd delayed him going to work this morning.

She decided to give him another half hour before seeking him out. Selecting a book from the Grand's library, she sat down on a sofa in the lobby. The clatter of silverware still came from the dining room where guests finished a late dinner. The noise distracted her from the pages so she was gazing around the deserted lobby when Cora approached.

"Miss Hinkle?" Ned's younger cousin addressed her.

"Please, call me Bethany."

"Thank you. It's really not my place to tell you this, but I noticed you seem to be waiting for someone. Ned?"

"Yes," Bethany responded, feeling a little heat in her cheeks.

"Were you aware that there were problems on the golf course?"

"What kind of problems?" Anxiety rose in her.

"Someone destroyed the irrigation system last night."

"What?" Oh, God. A few nights ago, he'd been worried about the course. *Please don't let it be the Crusaders.*

"Ned's been working all day to fix it. I would imagine he's still there now. I thought you'd want to know."

"Yes, thank you."

Cora walked away, taking her post behind the massive reception desk.

Bethany had been concerned about not having a dance partner, while he was struggling to fix the complex irrigation system. She felt selfish and petty, and just a little guilty. There must be something she could do to help him.

Bethany strode up to the counter. "Is there someone who can take me to—"

Cora was already reaching for the phone. "Yauncey's still available. He'll meet you out front."

Bethany should have changed out of the black cocktail dress and silver heels she'd worn to dinner, but she didn't want to take the time. After the short drive to the golf course, she stepped into the room that housed the irrigation system. Ned worked at a temporary table, strewn with components. An uneaten meal from the dining room lay in a takeout container amongst the tools. The control panel leaned against the wall, gaping open and empty.

"Ned," she said softly, afraid of making him jump. He was so focused on his task.

He whirled around, staring at her, his face bewildered, his hair sticking up. He wore the same clothes as he had last evening.

"What do you want?" he demanded hoarsely.

"Cora just told me what happened." She wanted to go to him and wrap her arms around him, but she hesitated, unsure what to do. "I'm so sorry. Is there anything I can do?"

"Yeah, you can skip the innocent act and get the hell off my golf course."

"Innocent act?" She took a step back, cursing her connection with the Crusaders. "You think I had something to do with this?"

"I've known all along you work for the Crusaders." His words were bitter. "But you got me—you got me good. I totally fell for your performance. Was sleeping with me part of your plan to snow me, make sure I didn't suspect you?"

"I didn't do this," she insisted. How could he think that after what they'd shared?

"Not with your own hands, but you fed your employer information about my golf course."

She closed her eyes. She had told Paul about this room and the sophisticated irrigation system it housed. What if he told others at the Crusader's office?

"You did," he accused. "At least I can read that on your face since you've been able to fool me about everything else."

"I wasn't trying to fool you, and I wasn't sleeping with you for any reason other than I wanted to."

"Like hell. Now go." He turned back to his work. He ignored her as he traced his finger across a schematic and adjusted the part in his hands.

"Would you stop and talk to me?" she pleaded with him. He had to listen to her. This was all nonsense.

"No time, but you knew that too." He tossed his tools down and stalked toward her, backing her against the wall. "You knew I have the chance to host a tournament here if the course passes inspection tomorrow. Oh, yeah, you planned well, but I'm going to beat you at your own game. I'm going to get this system working again by morning. So your plan to damage my course's reputation is going to fail."

"Ned, I had nothing—" She tried again to defend herself. He had it all wrong.

"My question is why? Why target me and my course? I'm actually in compliance unlike half the damn courses in Georgia. Why do the Crusaders have a beef with me?"

She could answer that. Tell him some truth, and then maybe he'd believe her about the vandalism. "We, the Crusaders I mean, targeted the twenty most successful courses in the state. Courses where the wealthy play. Causing trouble for those places has the most impact on policy."

His eyes widened in disbelief. "Christ, your own father plays here," he bellowed at her.

"I didn't make the selections and I never vandalized anything." She tried to make him understand. "I sent letters and emails, did research about compliance. That was my role. And for the record. I don't work for the Crusaders anymore."

"Yeah? Since when? Your picture's on their website."

"I quit last month before I even came here."

"So you told them nothing about my course?"

Damn it. He had her there. She swallowed. "I did speak with my former boss after I saw your operation and I told him I thought it was clean. But, please hear me, I'm done working for them."

"What I don't understand is why you ever did."

"Because I give a shit about the environment," she raised her voice. "That's why I worked for the Crusaders. To make a difference so kids don't drink water laced with chemicals, so run-off doesn't go into the ocean. Golf courses are huge polluters of ground water." She stood taller. With her heels on, she was eye-to-eye with him.

"I'm aware of that," he snapped. "It's the reason I spent over a million dollars this year alone upgrading my procedures and equipment. Equipment that your asshole co-workers took a hammer to."

"Former co-workers," she clarified again.

"Get out of here." He took a step away from her. "I've got work to do."

She squared her shoulders and stalked to the door. Although she hadn't been totally honest with him, this incident wasn't her fault. She was shaking with emotion when she got to the van.

"Back to the hotel, Miss?" Yauncey asked when he opened the door for her.

"Give me a minute," she said, climbing into the vehicle and swiping at her tears. Anger, frustration, and, she had to admit it, sadness—all reasons to cry—raged inside her. "Thank you." She accepted the tissue box from the hotel employee.

Yauncey got in behind the wheel and waited. "Miss Bethany, is there anything I can do?"

She thought for a second, trying to see the situation objectively. She couldn't process yet what she'd lost, but she could think clearly enough to know what she had to do. She took in a shaky breath. "Yes, you can take me to the police station in the village."

If her picture was on the Crusader's website, the images of the vandals were there too. She could point out the two employees involved in the previous vandalism and give the name and information about the man fired from the Crusaders.

She could do that for Ned, whether he wanted her help or not.

****

"I've got the first round, Chuck, and the second," Ned said. He owed his work crew and the hotel's maintenance guys more than some pitchers of beer, but it was a quick way of showing his thanks. He'd make sure their Christmas bonus checks were extra generous as well.

"We did it," Rob congratulated him, taking a seat at the bar. "God, I'm tired."

"It's a frickin' miracle," Grant said from Ned's other side.

The irrigation system was operational again by four in the morning and the other damage erased from the course. Ned had stumbled home, fallen into bed for two hours, showered, and returned to the club house to meet the tournament representatives. He'd spent the day showing off his course and talking up the recent improvements. In the evening, he'd dined with the two tournament representatives in the hotel's main dining room, which was an easy way to display the quality and atmosphere of the Grand. He'd wanted them to imagine golfers and their entourages relaxing in the splendor of the resort.

Intentionally, he'd seated himself with his back to the other diners to avoid seeing Bethany. She'd be beautiful, dressed for dinner with her family, but she was the reason he'd been in such a jam today. She'd sold him out. It didn't matter how much he wanted her, he couldn't trust her.

"We'll know for sure soon," Ned said to join in the banter. He was hopeful about his chances. That was the good news of the day. When the representatives were departing, they indicated that he could expect to be hosting an event next fall.

"Ellen'll pump them for information on the hop to the mainland. They'll be at her mercy in that little plane." Grant held up his hand and tipped it to indicate a diving plane.

"Christ, she did that to me once when she was mad. Damn near lost my lunch," Pete McCormack, Ellen's longtime friend, joined the group at the bar.

"Hey, Ned," one of his crew called from behind him. Ned swiveled on his bar stool to face the table of Grand employees. "Jackson says they caught the bastards this afternoon."

Jackson, a retired cop from the mainland, worked an occasional shift for the White Pine Island Police Department. The gray haired officer had taken a seat with Ned's employees and helped himself to a glass of beer.

"They were still on the island?" Ned assumed they would have left on the first ferry yesterday.

"Yeah, they'd been camping up in the woods. Lots of places to hide on the island's center." Jackson gulped down his beer. "Today, they were trying to bum a ride with some fishermen when the chief spotted them. He recognized the guys from the witness's description and when he searched them—"

"What witness?" Ned interrupted him.

"A woman. I thought she was one of your guests." Jackson wrinkled up his forehead. "She showed up late last night when I was on duty and gave a statement."

Ned pictured Bethany as she'd appeared the evening before, beautiful and angry. She'd gone to the police after leaving him? That didn't make sense. "Black dress, dark hair, tall?" Ned asked to confirm it was Bethany.

"That's her. Good looking woman." Jackson grinned.

"Did the chief make an arrest?" Grant had swiveled around as well.

"Last I heard he was verifying the fingerprints, but the guys had cans of spray paint in their bags and a crow bar that was probably used to pry open the door and smash stuff up."

"Got the bastards," Grant exclaimed, clapping a hand on Ned's shoulder. "Now that's something to drink to." Grant raised his glass in celebration. "Next round's on me, Chuck."

An hour and three beers later, Ned still sat on the bar stool. The crew drank a couple pitchers of beer and headed home, leaving only Grant and Pete as his company. Ned had thought about leaving. He needed to sleep, but he needed a lot more alcohol before that was going to happen. Enough beer might erase the images of Bethany that he couldn't get out of his mind.

"So who's this guest who was the witness?" Pete asked as round four arrived.

"Bethany Hinkle," Grant answered for him and Ned grunted.

"Should I know her?" Pete scratched his jaw, thinking.

"No," Ned said, "and I advise you to stay away from her. She's trouble."

"Yeah? She helped the cops catch the bad guys," Pete said with a shrug. "Doesn't sound like trouble to me. I think I'd thank her."

Pete probably would. He was too damn nice sometimes. Expressing gratitude to Bethany was about the last thing Ned planned to do.

The bar's door swung open. The click of high heels and giggling invaded the quiet space as five women walked in. Priscilla Hinkle led the way, wearing a tiara and a white sash with *Bride to Be* written on it in pink glitter. Three beauty queen types came next, each with a pink tiara on her head. Bethany entered the bar last, wearing a *Bride's Little Sister* ball cap and a worried frown.

"Here's your chance to thank her, Pete," Grant said, nodding to the women.

"Ellen told me there was a wedding this weekend. I guess that's it," Peter said in a low voice. "High maintenance types. Which one's Bethany?"

"The last one," Ned muttered. She hadn't spotted him yet so he had a chance to observe her. She looked out-of-place and a little miserable as she trailed after the other women to a corner booth.

"Huh," Pete said, evaluating her. "Pretty enough. What's the problem?"

"Can't trust her," Ned said, drinking half his beer.

"You aren't interested, are you?" Grant dug into Pete, the two of them keeping their eyes on the booth.

"Not my type."

"Ah, shit." Grant muttered under his breath to Ned. "One of the bridesmaids is making eyes in our direction. I'm getting the come hither look." Laughter came from the booth, along with some catcalls.

"Go over there at your own peril," Ned commented. "I'm not moving."

"I want nothing to do with that table. You're on your own, Grant. See you all later." Pete tossed a few bucks on the bar and headed for the door.

"You've been spotted," Grant warned, turning back toward the bar. "Ex-girlfriend at six o'clock."

Three seconds later, she slid onto the stool abandoned by Pete. Her leg bumped into Ned's as she turned toward him. He tried to ignore the ripple of awareness that went through him.

"Miss Hinkle," he greeted her, like he would any guest of his family's hotel.

"Hi, Ned," she said, her voice wary. "I wanted to ask how it went today with the tournament people. I saw you with them at dinner and...." She'd removed the silly hat, letting her shiny hair loose.

"Fine," he said, his jaw locked tight.

Her fingers tapped against the bar and she sighed. She was uncomfortable, hell, so was he. She should have stayed at her table or stayed the hell out of a local bar. Tourists, especially bachelorette parties, didn't come to Chuck's.

"Would you give us a minute, please?" she said to Grant.

"Not a problem," his cousin responded before strolling over to the bachelorette party table.

Bethany's cool demeanor irritated Ned, but he wasn't getting into a fight with her in a bar. If he was honest with himself, he had no reason to fight with her at all. He'd said what he needed to say already. A week from now, she'd be gone from the island and his life.

He should be happy about that, but the thought of not seeing her again left him empty inside.

"I came over to apologize," she said, speaking softly. "I never meant to cause you any problems, and I thought I was helping you."

He looked her in the face for the first time since she took a seat. "By reporting about my course to the Crusaders?"

"I know it seems counterintuitive, but—"

"Damn right it does." He tilted his head toward the table that was getting louder every minute. "You should get back to your party."

She stared at him for a minute, her eyes glinting like blue fire.

"Okay. I'll go, but there's one thing I can't figure out." Her hair brushed against his shoulder as she leaned closer to him. "If you knew I worked for the Crusaders, why'd you let me get close to you?"

"Keep your friends close and your enemies closer," he said quickly and regretted it just as fast when tears sprang to her eyes.

Chapter Ten

"I can't play dress up this afternoon," Bethany said for the second time in three minutes. "I have some place I need to be."

"Not with Ned I assume. He dropped you cold." Priscilla rubbed salt in Bethany's open wound, a wound that hadn't healed even a tiny bit in the two days since she'd seen him.

His words at the bar had stabbed her, gone straight to her core. Even now, she flinched and rubbed a hand over her heart just thinking about them. She'd gotten back to the table, stuck the hideous ball cap on her head to hide her tears and tucked herself in the corner of the booth. Priscilla's friends weren't interested in her anyway so no one asked about her encounter with the guy at the bar. When they left Chuck's, she pleaded a headache and got a taxi to the hotel. No one missed her company then, nor would they today.

"You don't need me for this," Bethany insisted.

Priscilla wanted to do a "dry-run" of the hair and makeup for the wedding to see how the look would photograph. Bethany had endured a bridesmaid luncheon yesterday, followed by cocktails with the entire bridal party. Another get-together required her attendance this evening, and tomorrow would be the rehearsal dinner. Bethany planned to have her own celebration when this blessed wedding was over.

"I knew I shouldn't have asked you to be a bridesmaid. You just don't understand. Mom." Priscilla turned to their mother, expecting support for her cause.

"Can't you change your plans, honey?" Her mother usually took Priscilla's side because it was easier than listening to her eldest child complain, so Bethany wasn't surprised by the question.

"No, I can't." Yesterday, while the other bridesmaids were in the spa, she'd managed to sneak off to a second interview with Dr. Monroe at the research center. Only two candidates remained for the position, and she was one of them. The next hurdle was an interview with the board. This afternoon.

Under normal circumstances, a meeting with the people who might hire her would be nerve-wracking. Remembering that Ned was on the research center's board made it closer to terrifying. After what he said to her and the blame and anger he'd heaped on her, she'd have to rely on every ounce of composure she could summon.

"Ridiculous," Priscilla yelled, her princess persona cracking. "Daddy!"

Bethany turned to her father, who lounged on the sofa in her parents' suite, watching the exchange between the sisters. Her father had often championed her, but this was Priscilla's wedding so she wasn't expecting any help from him today.

When they were alone this morning at breakfast, her father did ask her about Ned. But she couldn't make herself explain the complicated situation between them. She'd just shaken her head, tears too close to the surface at the mention of their intense, but short-lived relationship.

And Ned would be across the table from her today, making a decision about her employment.

"Daddy!" Priscilla squealed again when their father didn't react to her first plea.

"Perhaps, your sister could understand your absence better if you said where you're going and where you went yesterday afternoon. I was playing golf and saw you bike off on the loop road."

Great. An inquisition. She wanted to ask if he'd been golfing with Ned, but didn't dare bring up his name. Priscilla would jump all over that.

"I know you're an adult, Bethie, but I'm worried about you," her father continued.

"I'm fine." She took a deep breath. She hadn't wanted to tell them about her interviews for fear she wouldn't get the job. With the three of them staring at her, it was silly to conceal it any longer so she plunged ahead. "I had a job interview, a second one actually, yesterday."

"Thank goodness," her mother exclaimed. "I've been hoping you'd quit that environmental place."

"I already did, mom. I don't have a job at the moment, and I need this position."

"On the island? Where?" her father asked.

"The marine research center. It's a research assistantship."

"To study what? Fish?" Priscilla's tone was mocking. "Here?"

"I like fish, Priscilla, and I like being on this island and not only for a fancy vacation."

"You quit your job?" Her father wanted her to confirm.

"I know I shouldn't have until I got another one, but I can find some way to support myself if this doesn't work. I may even stay on the island and get a job somewhere else."

"What, as a waitress or cashier?" Priscilla demanded.

"If I need to. I'm tired of accepting handouts from my parents. It's time to be independent." Bethany targeted her sister. Priscilla had milked their parents for everything, starting from when she was a little girl. Her extravagant wedding was just another example.

"A full-time research position. That sounds like just the sort of thing you'd like." Her father's words put an end to Priscilla's outbursts, but not her sneer.

"It's down to two candidates," Bethany explained. "The final choice rests with the center's board and today is an interview with the board members."

"Have you prepared?" Her father asked, ignoring Priscilla's pouting.

"As much as I can," Bethany admitted, unsure of how to face Ned across the table. "I don't know what to expect."

Her father nodded. "Meet me in the lobby in ten minutes. We'll run through some possible questions." Her father's experience in business could be a life-saver when it came to this interview. She couldn't expect Ned to vote in her favor, so she had to win over the other four board members. With any luck, he wouldn't blackball her employment.

****

"You want to grab lunch?" Grant caught up to Ned as he strode across the course. "I've got an hour before my next program."

"Nah, not hungry." Ned kept walking toward the pro shop.

"That's the second day in a row you turned down food. Or is it me?" Grant grinned.

"I've got to cut out early for a board meeting at the marine research center. I need to finish some things before I go." Dr. Monroe was finally ready to hire the assistantship. He'd narrowed a field of nearly one hundred applicants to two. Since the grant required that the new researcher be hired by tomorrow, the board had to meet, interview, and vote, all in one shot.

"Since it's technically your day off, you can't have that much to do." Grant pointed out.

Ned shrugged. He'd skipped his weekly day off. Working was easier than thinking about who he'd spent his day off with last week. Before everything went to shit, he'd made plans to take her back to the plantation house and show her the interior. Or they could have biked around the island, gone to the winery or simply spent the day in his bed.

"You aren't love sick, are you?" Grant asked, a note of disgust in his voice.

"I'm busy."

"Have you seen her?" Grant wasn't going to let it go.

"Not since the bar the other night. I was such a dick." He'd cut himself off from her by his angry words. Even if he went to her, she'd probably refuse to see him.

"You're just feeling guilty. Remember what she did to you."

"Yeah, that's what I've been thinking about." He yanked the door of the pro shop open and headed for his office. "What did she really do to me?"

"She gave her boss information about your course, which resulted in vandalism," Grant argued, following him into the building.

"Vandalism wasn't her intent." He was sure of that now, especially since she'd supplied descriptions of possible suspects to the police.

"Maybe not, but it sure screwed you over."

He'd lost some sleep over the damage and money, which the insurance company would reimburse. He was losing a lot more sleep over the way things ended between Bethany and him.

"I got a call from the Crusaders yesterday. An apology call."

Grant plopped into a chair. "Unexpected, but nice."

"I talked to the director. He fired the guys who hit my course, and he turned over evidence to indict them on previous attacks."

"So the place has some redeeming qualities. Did you ask about Bethany's role in this?"

"I didn't have to ask. He offered. Other than sending some pictures to him, she had nothing to do with the vandalism." Her boss had confirmed that she'd quit last month although he'd begged her to stay. The director couldn't say enough flattering things about her dedication and work ethic.

Grant studied him for a moment. "So you're convinced of her innocence and you want to patch things up with her?"

"I don't know. She's not going to want to see me, and she'll leave the island soon anyway. The best I can hope for is a chance to apologize." She was scheduled to check out on Sunday. He'd logged into the Grand's reservation system and confirmed that.

"Is that really going to be enough?"

His cousin knew him too well. It wasn't enough. Nothing but getting back to where they'd been a few days ago was going to be enough.

"No," Ned said. He wanted another chance with her, but he wasn't sure he'd get it.

"I saw her on the porch last evening at some pre-wedding party. I think she's caught up with Priscilla's wedding." Was his cousin trying to find a nice way of discouraging him? "She looked totally hot." Grant shot him a grin.

Ned laughed for the first time in days. The wedding couldn't take up every minute of her time from now until Sunday. And he'd be damned if he'd let her leave this island without a conversation.

"I guess I'll have to do battle with the princess to get a few minutes with Bethany."

He'd wanted to seek Bethany out right then, but he had to get through this board meeting first. He'd parked in front of the research center and rushed inside, already late. Dr. Monroe handed him a packet of information about the first candidate, and he reviewed it at lightning speed before the interview started.

The man was a recent graduate of Florida State University with a degree in environmental science. He had excellent academic credentials, seemed capable, but had little work experience. Not a bad choice, but Ned was hoping for someone more dynamic. He chatted with the other board members between the interviews and found they agreed with him.

"I think you'll like our second candidate a little more," Dr. Monroe said, handing out a manila folder to each person at the table. "She would be my choice, but I wanted to bring the top two to your attention."

Ned flipped open the folder and froze. *Bethany Hinkle* were the first words he read. He kept his head down, pretending to study the information, but his mind was spinning. Did she know he was on the board? Was that one of the reasons she'd pursued a relationship with him? His plans to seek her out later today evaporated.

"She has more work experience. An environmental group which makes sense for our research," one of the board members said.

"And she volunteered here as a teenager when her family was vacationing on the island."

She had? He didn't know that about her, maybe he didn't know a lot of things about her. He reviewed what he did know about her career goals. She'd said she was pursuing a change to work in her field of marine biology. She'd made no secret of that. What if she hadn't told him about her interviews here because she didn't want his help getting this job?

"I'll bring her in," Dr. Monroe said.

Ned's mouth went dry when she walked in the room. In a cream-colored dress, she was beautiful and professional as she smiled and shook hands with each board member during introductions.

Without hesitation, she took Ned's hand. "It's good to see you again, Mr. Phillips," she greeted him, acknowledging a connection between them before moving on to the next person.

He wanted to grab hold of her and never let go. He'd already made the mistake of not trusting her. He wasn't doing that again.

****

Bethany silently thanked her father for his tutorial this morning. She'd confessed the disastrous end to her relationship with Ned and told her father that Ned sat on the board. Her father advised she greet him as an old friend. Trying to hide they knew each other was the wrong approach. Get the white elephant out in the open, he'd insisted.

She'd done exactly that while Ned's hand possessed hers. His expression was a little stunned before changing to one she couldn't read.

Over the next half-hour, she answered the board's questions, talked about her experience working for the Crusaders, and explained why she left that job. She switched her gaze from member to member as she spoke.

Ned only met her eyes when she recounted what led her to quit the Crusaders. She emphasized that the group had become too radical for her tastes and strayed from their real mission of helping the environment. For one second, she thought he might interject, but he said nothing.

"We'll be in touch, Miss Hinkle." Dr. Monroe signaled the end of her interview. "As you know, we have to make our decision soon."

"Thank you," she said, standing up as the others rose. "It was a pleasure to meet you all."

She kept her composure until she got outside and walked away from the building. Slowly, she released the tension in her shoulders as she stood in the bright afternoon sunshine. She needed a few minutes to unwind.

Blowing out a deep breath, she made her way to a bench where she could see the ocean and calm her racing heart. Being near Ned did things to her that she couldn't explain, made her want things she'd never considered.

But it was over between them.

She sighed, shifting her attention to her surroundings where she might find some solace. The Atlantic was deep blue and tranquil this afternoon under a cloudless sky. She'd love to see this view every day, live on White Pine Island, and be where she might glimpse Ned, even if it was only on the golf course.

With a little shake of her head, she dismissed her pipe dream. She had to return to the reality of her sister's wedding so she picked up her phone to call the Grand Hotel's front desk. Taking her mother's advice, she'd worn a slim-fitting cream sheath dress so biking was out of the question. Now, she had to depend on Yauncey to come get her.

"Can I give you a lift?" Ned said from just behind her, causing her back to stiffen. "I think we're headed the same way."

"I was just calling...." She held her phone so he could see.

"Let's save Yauncey the trip." He sat with her, resting his arm along the bench's back right behind her shoulders.

"If you don't mind," she said reluctantly. "Thank you."

For a moment, only the sounds of the sea filled the air around them. She kept her eyes on the water, not sure what to make of his company.

"In case you're wondering," he broke the silence, "the board voted already. Four to zero in your favor."

"I got the job!" She turned toward him, excited, but it didn't last. "Wait. There are five board members."

"I abstained," he said.

"Oh. I see." Very professional of him, she thought, since he couldn't be objective about her. He must despise her as much as she feared.

"I had to, but I did wait to make sure the vote was going in your favor before abstaining."

"I appreciate your integrity," she said, keeping her voice level. "Maybe I should call for Yauncey. I'm sure he'll—"

"It has nothing to do with integrity," Ned cut her off. "I was concerned about conflict of interest. It would be tough to explain to the other board members why I was kissing our new research assistant."

"Kissing?" Had one of the board members seen them together and raised an objection?

"*If* you can forgive me." His fingers dropped to her shoulder, drawing tiny circles against her skin.

He was talking about the future, not the past.

"I'm sorry for blaming you. I should never have done that, but I can't forgive myself for what I said to you, the way I said it, in the bar." His fingers stilled. "Bethany, I have to be upfront. There's some truth to that or was. I did plan to get close to you to watch what you were doing. It was a stupid idea and I—"

"How long did you pretend?" she asked, not wanting to think he was faking when he first kissed her at the plantation house.

"Until the afternoon we went paddling. Only one day. When that big wave took you under...." he shook his head. "After that, everything...everything was real."

She closed her eyes for a second, enjoying the sunshine on her face. Everything she felt for him was real, too. If they could find a way forward....

"So now?" She met his gaze and saw the hope she felt reflected in his dark eyes.

"To start with, I'd like to keep a promise to you." He pulled an old iron key from his pocket. "I said that I'd take you inside the plantation house. We could go now."

"I'd like that, but first," she said, standing and pulling him to his feet, "I want to make sure you abstained for a reason." She clasped her hands behind his neck and tugged his head down toward hers.

His arms surrounded her, holding her tight against him, as their lips met in the sunshine of White Pine Island.

~The End~

A Note from the Author

Thank you for reading Ned and Bethany's story from *Christmas at the Grand Hotel*. I hope you enjoyed it! Please look for the next three books in the series throughout 2017. *Springtime at the Grand Hotel, Summer at the Grand Hotel*, and *Autumn at the Grand Hotel*.

If you enjoyed my work, please visit me at www.maywilliams.com to learn about my other novels.

Animal Prints

Snow Prints

Finger Prints

Playing for His Heart

Dressed for Love – A Victorian Trilogy

I would love to hear from you or connect with you on social media. Please follow me on twitter @maywilliams2 or find me on facebook.

Happy Reading and Merry Christmas!

May Williams

Christmas at the Grand Hotel

White Pine Island: Novella Two
Ellen & Pete

by

Amie Denman

Copyright 2016 by Amie Denman
Christmas at the Grand Hotel
White Pine Island: Novella Two
Ellen & Pete

All rights reserved. The unauthorized reproduction or distribution of this copyrighted work, in whole or part, by any electronic, mechanical, or other means, is illegal and forbidden.

This is a work of fiction. Characters, settings, names, and occurrences are a product of the author's imagination and bear no resemblance to any actual person, living or dead, places or settings, and/or occurrences. Any incidences of resemblance are purely coincidental.

Chapter One

Pete McCormack leaned on a rail and watched the White Pine Island Ferry nudge the dock. A deckhand threw a thick rope over a post and secured it. A quiet Thursday evening in mid December, this was the last ferry of the day. He waited, enjoying the sound of the waves lapping against the shore. After a long day of renting golf carts to tourists, making repairs, and overseeing his family's business, he was ready to call it a night.

But he needed the package from the mainland, a part for one of his golf carts with electrical problems. And seeing the ferry captain, his best friend since kindergarten, was a nice way to cap off a day.

Christmas lights decorated the dock and the houses on the bluff above the water. On top of the hill behind him, the Georgia pines lining the long driveway of the Grand Hotel twinkled with red and green lights.

A night insect buzzed past. A boat horn sounded. A petite woman with a long blonde ponytail strode across the deck. She wore dark blue pants, a white shirt, and a captain's hat.

"Got your box of switches and wires from the hardware store," she said, handing him a clipboard to sign. "Your golf cart will live another day."

"Not if the tourists keep beating them up," he lamented. "I have no idea how someone tore out the turn signal wires."

"Make them put down a giant deposit. You're too nice. Always have been."

"It's a horrible character flaw," he said. "I'll try to change."

Ellen wrinkled her nose at him. "Don't do that. You know I hate change."

The Atlantic Ocean lapped gently at the dock. Almost four miles away, lights on the Georgia coast twinkled. From the strip of tourist bars and restaurants just up the hill, Pete heard music and laughter.

But it seemed as if he was alone with Ellen Phillips. The girl who had been at his fingertips but out of reach his entire life. White Pine Island only had one school and one church. Ellen had sat next to him in math class, across from him at graduation, and just down the pew when their high school friends got married one by one. They'd also shared food and drinks with other locals, enjoying the fun and freedom of growing up on a resort island with warm weather year round.

Ellen tilted her head and her ponytail slid over one shoulder. In the glow from the Christmas lights, he saw her draw her eyebrows together and grin at him. "You know I'm off the clock right now, so you should sign for your parts so I can go home."

Pete laughed. "You're never off the clock when you work for the family business. Neither am I."

"No one rents a golf cart at night."

"True, but that's when I charge batteries, buff out scuffs, update our social media, and make my marketing plan for world golf cart rental domination."

She laughed. "I'm headed up the hill to impose my will on a bottle of wine I swiped out of the cellar. I'm celebrating."

"What are you celebrating?"

"I finally have almost enough flight hours to qualify for a commercial pilot's license. I only need three more hours and I can sit for the exam."

"I thought you'd been flying commercial for years for the hotel."

She shook her head. "Not exactly. I had a private pilot's license, so my parents couldn't pay me for ferrying people and cargo from the mainland to the hotel. They just generously allowed me to fly the Grand Hotel plane and help them out. With a commercial license, I have a lot more options."

Pete felt his heart sink. "With a boat captain's license and a pilot's license, I'm surprised you don't sail or fly away from this island."

Ellen punched him lightly in the gut. "I do that all the time, but I always come back. This island is home. Where else could I find a good friend like you?"

Friend. And the most interesting thing I drive all day long is a six-seater golf cart.

"You look serious," Ellen said. "Is something bothering you?"

He'd tried hiding things from Ellen before. Like the time he'd found her cat run over in the long graceful driveway of her family's Grand Hotel. He was delivering newspapers on his bike. He'd scooped the cat into a newspaper and put it in his bike's basket, desperate to buy time and think of a way to tell her. But she knew there was something wrong as soon as she saw his face. He remembered holding her in his arms as she cried on his shoulder. They were eleven years old. Could it really be fourteen years ago?

There would never be a good time to tell her what was on his mind, but he couldn't do it tonight. Not with the gentle salt air and holiday spirit everywhere.

"It's late," he said. "How about a ride up the hill?"

She unfurrowed her brow, but her expression still suggested she had questions to ask.

"I have to lock up the wheelhouse and check the lines again, but then I'll take you up on that ride. The holiday rush has started, and I'm conserving my energy."

Pete stowed the box of electrical parts on the back seat of his golf cart and climbed in the driver's seat to wait for Ellen. His fingers itched to start his wiring job, to do something that challenged his mind. This familiarity, this sameness, was the reason he always wanted to get away from the island. But it was also the reason he wanted to stay.

"Almost ready," she called from the upper deck of the ferry. Pete wiped the dew from the seat next to him and waited. He heard Ellen thundering down the metal staircase and crossing the boat with her quick step. She slid in next to him, bumping shoulders and not bothering to scoot away.

"Where to?" he asked jovially.

She laughed. "Home. I started early today flying a couple of guests to Savannah. And then I took extra shifts running the ferry so Jimmy could go to his daughter's Christmas party at school."

"You should talk your family into hiring an additional boat captain so you don't have to put in such long days."

"I love piloting the ferry. And I promised my parents and my aunt and uncle I'd be in charge of it when they bought the ferry service a few years ago. The only drawback is that I probably smell like engines, fish, and sweat," Ellen said.

Pete smiled. "You smell fine. Like the ocean as usual."

He kept his eyes on the darkened road ahead of him, but he knew the moment her head jerked around to look at him. Maybe he shouldn't have mentioned he knew her scent. Even though their thighs were touching and their elbows knocked together in the close quarters of the golf cart, Ellen could never be any closer to him than a friend. A very good friend. A friend who made him toss and turn with unanswered questions in his lonely room above the golf rental business. He'd moved out of his parent's house, but he hadn't gone far. Couldn't go far.

If there ever was a time he and Ellen could have moved beyond friendship, it was past. And there wouldn't be another chance.

"My family went nuts with the holiday decorating at the Hotel this year," Ellen said. "I'm glad I've been too busy flying and ferrying guests to get roped into hanging lights on trees. It's not my thing."

Pete laughed. "I know. I remember one time they tried to get you to help decorate the ballroom for a wedding. You set up ladders for the housekeeping staff and then went and hid in the woods."

"I'm not much of a decorator," she admitted. "But I like seeing the lights." She sighed. "I love Christmas. Have you seen the massive tree we put up in the lobby?"

"Not yet."

"We should stop by and take a peek on the way to my house," Ellen suggested. "Unless you're in a hurry."

"No hurry."

He turned onto the road that led across the front of the imposing white structure. The Grand Hotel had stood on a bluff overlooking the island for a century. With its five course meals, formal attire, and designer-decorated rooms, it set the standard for gracious accommodations and was the finest hotel on the island. Pete knew the story. Ellen's grandparents had bought the hotel decades ago, passed it to their children, and she and her siblings and their cousins were next in line. She was practically island royalty.

And his parents had just decided to sell their twenty-year-old family business catering to tourists who wanted to careen around the island on a rented golf cart. His father's medical problems had been a bitter warning that life is short, and his parents were ready to do what they always said they would—move to a little place on the mainland. They'd be close to Pete's older sister who'd gone to college and never returned to White Pine Island.

Without being tied to the family business, he would no longer feel the weight of responsibility he'd felt for his aging parents. He'd be free.

"Everyone will be finishing dinner and then heading in to listen to the orchestra," Ellen said, still on the subject of the holiday decorations at the Grand Hotel. "No one will see us in our crappy work clothes."

"Hey," Pete said. "These cargo shorts still have almost all the belt loops and this is one of my best t-shirts. You, however, look like you work on a cruise ship instead of being the heir to the local throne."

"I'll put on my heiress costume for the holiday party," Ellen said. "Tonight, we're sneaking in to look at decorations and maybe steal something good from the kitchen."

"Just like old times."

He had to tell her soon, but not tonight. Her smile was lit by the colorful lights as he parked at the far end of the porch. She giggled as they dashed through the kitchen entrance and slipped into the lobby. A two-story Christmas tree stood at one end and sparkled with decorations. Tables, plush furniture, and several smaller trees were scattered in groups on the floral carpeting.

"What do you think of the tree?" she asked. Pete glanced at her shining face. Even though she was the resident tomboy of the Grand Hotel, he knew she felt all the Phillips pride in the place and would be a gracious hostess when her time to run the hotel came. Her future had always been clear to her. Along with her generation of the family, Ellen was already taking a role in running the place. Her siblings and cousins managed recreation, special events, the golf course, and other amenities. Ellen was all about transportation, an area the Phillips family took seriously because they would have no business if guests couldn't get to the island.

Pete shaded his eyes and looked around. "What tree? I can't see anything with all these damn twinkling lights."

Ellen elbowed him and scooped up several chocolates from a bowl on a nearby table. She held out her hand with the gold-foil wrapped candies. "Your favorites. It's my cab fare for my ride home."

"You know I can't resist these." Pete took two chocolates from her warm palm.

"Just don't leave them in your pocket when you do laundry."

Pete laughed. "I haven't done that in years."

He was surprised she remembered. But then again he remembered all kinds of little things about her. Her December birthday that was coming up and was always overshadowed by Christmas. The fact that eating peppermints made her sneeze. Her absolute aversion to country music even though they lived in Georgia. The way their mutual friend Alex had crumpled up her heart and tossed it in the ocean when he left the island five years ago and never came back.

He doubted he would ever know anyone as well as he knew Ellen. Or love anyone as much.

"Ready to go?" he asked. He was getting sentimental. Maybe it was thinking about the changes coming up, perhaps it was the holidays. Either way, he needed to call it a night.

"More than ready. The wine's calling my name. I can hear it all the way from my cottage."

On the way through the kitchen, Ellen persuaded the kitchen staff to scoop two servings of seafood pasta into a foil pan.

"If we hurry, this will still be warm when we get to my place and you can come in and help me eat it," she said.

Pete had shared hundreds of meals with Ellen going back to kindergarten. Of course she would invite him in to eat. But for the first time in years, he considered saying no.

****

It had taken Ellen Phillips all the way to the eleventh grade before she realized she was pretty. She was halfway through senior year when she discovered she could date almost any boy on the island she wanted.

But she didn't want that. It was a lot more fun to be friends. To swim in the ocean without feeling awkward in a bathing suit. Share food and drinks without being on a date. To give and receive birthday presents and Christmas presents with no strings attached. This had been her relationship with almost everyone in her graduating class who'd grown up on the island, all twelve or so of them. She had only made the mistake of crossing the line once, and she'd paid for that, nursing a broken heart for months.

Her rock was always Pete. She didn't feel self-conscious in a swimsuit in front of him and she had never dated him. But his birthday gifts were just what she wanted. His text messages were usually just what she needed to hear.

And their lifelong understanding of each other was the reason Ellen knew something was not the same tonight. Pete always drove with one hand slung over the wheel. Tonight, he gripped it with both hands as if he was afraid he would lose control on a road he'd driven a thousand times.

"I hope you haven't already had dinner," Ellen said.

"Mom made her famous lasagna tonight," Pete said. Ellen laughed. "I'm sorry to hear it."

"Not as sorry as my dad. I told them I couldn't stay for dinner because I had to meet the ferry. I'm sure Mom will freeze leftovers for me anyway."

"Your poor dog."

"Don't worry about him," Pete said. "I don't even try to make Edison eat my mother's cooking anymore. No one should have to do that."

"You know I have no idea what kind of a cook my mother is," Ellen said. "We always had whatever was being served in the dining room when I was a kid. And I still swing by and pilfer dinner."

"How much longer do you think you can get away with that?"

"Forever."

Pete cleared his throat but didn't say anything.

"No sense changing a good thing when you have it," Ellen added. Why was Pete so quiet tonight?

Pete's took one hand off the wheel and scrubbed it through his short dark hair. She'd seen him make that same nervous gesture on other occasions. The day they went to the mainland together to take the SAT test the fall of their senior year. The summer Sunday when he was best man at their friend Chuck's wedding. And a rainy spring day waiting outside the operating room to hear the surgeon's news about his father's cancer.

What was bothering him tonight?

They turned off the one-lane road and the golf cart's headlights illuminated a gravel drive. Pete pulled to a stop in front of a small wood-sided cottage.

"One of your porch lights is out," he said. "I could come by and fix that for you."

"I only need one," she said.

Pete gave her a sarcastic look. "And what will you do when that one goes out?"

"Use the flashlight app on my phone."

"I'll bring my volt meter tomorrow. I don't want you coming home to a dark house and stumbling around."

"I don't want to be a pain," Ellen protested.

Pete breathed loudly through his nose. "I have a degree in electrical engineering, and I've pretty much only used it for recharging batteries on golf carts. If I don't challenge myself at least a little, I'm afraid I'll forget everything I learned."

Was that the issue on his mind? Like her, Pete felt a strong sense of responsibility to his family. He'd gone to college online so he wouldn't have to leave the island. It took him a year longer to finish because he ran his parents' business during his father's health crisis. Now that his father was better, did Pete feel that he wasn't needed anymore?

Ellen held the foil pan carefully while she slid out of the golf cart. She handed Pete the tray as she unlocked her door and flipped the light switch inside. The one story cottage just up the hill from the hotel had been hers for several years. Her brother Ned had a similar one closer to the edge of the immense golf course the Grand Hotel maintained for its guests. Although they loved working with and for their family, both of them felt the need for personal space. Ned got his own place as soon as he completed the two-year college program in golf course management. Ellen skipped college, preferring to get a license to fly a plane and run a passenger ferry. Easton was still in college, but Ellen knew he'd find a place on the island when he finished instead of moving back into his childhood bedroom. Only her older sister Kate had left the island, and Ellen missed her every day.

"Have a seat. I'll throw this on plates and grab the wine."

She gestured toward the couch and coffee table that had once been used in the lobby of her family's hotel. Pete had eaten many meals on that couch, even slept there on occasion when it got too late or they'd had too much to drink. He always sat on the same place on the couch and she'd come to think of it as Pete's spot.

The small house had a combined living room and kitchen area with a hallway separating a bedroom and bathroom. Almost all of her furniture was colorful but re-purposed, and she didn't mind. She spent most of her time in her plane, at the hotel, or on the ferry. Her parents lived behind the hotel in a much nicer home which Ellen and her brothers had already decided to arm-wrestle for when the time came.

Just thinking about change carved out a hollow in Ellen's chest. If she could freeze time and keep everything exactly as it was, she would do it. She loved flying the Grand Hotel's Cessna, piloting the island ferry, slipping on a dress once in a while and greeting guests at the front desk. She loved being with her parents and her brothers, walking the elegant halls of the hotel that would one day be hers. Loved visiting her grandparents in their home on the island and ferrying them over to the mainland for shopping trips.

It had always seemed like it was too good to be true. Too good to last.

Ellen retreated to the tiny kitchen area where she scooped the pasta onto two plates. She knew all the menus by heart. This was Thursday, the blue menu. Tomorrow's menu would be red, the food just a notch fancier for a Friday night when weekend hotel guests would be arriving. Ellen added forks to the repurposed plates with faded Grand Hotel script, and delivered them to the coffee table.

Pete smiled and looked hungrily at the food. He never turned down a good meal from the kitchens of the hotel. Neither did she. But they'd never eaten together in the hotel dining room except for the day of their high school graduation when her parents hosted a party for the entire graduating class of a dozen students. The long dining room with its mirrored columns, elegant chandeliers, and sparkling place settings saw guests every day of the year for breakfast and lunch buffets followed by a five-course dinner. Every other month, the entire Phillips family met there for lunch to discuss and review their hospitality business.

Eating with Pete was much less formal and was as comfortable as her favorite sweatshirt.

"Be right back," she said. Pete paused, fork in air, and Ellen laughed. "Dig in."

Ellen returned to the kitchen to retrieve a bottle of wine from the fridge. As she sorted through the drawer for the corkscrew, she replayed everything Pete had said—and not said—tonight. She thought of his pensive look, his hands gripped on the wheel, his comment about using his degree. Suddenly, the truth hit her.

She glanced over her shoulder and saw Pete's dark head on her couch and she knew what was bothering him. It was the thing she had feared for years.

Her best friend was leaving the island.

She'd known it would come some day. He'd always said he wanted to have his own electrical business. Fixing problems all over the island, repairing lamps and faulty outlets, even helping out at her family's hotel on occasion—what if it wasn't enough for him anymore?

And what if that took him away from her?

Pain constricted her lungs and her eyes stung. She leaned on her counter, corkscrew in hand, appetite gone. Just as she was certain that Pete had something huge weighing on his mind, something staggering to tell her, she was also certain she *did not want to hear it*. Couldn't face it tonight. Maybe not ever.

As she walked into the living room, a wine glass in each hand, Pete glanced up and smiled at her. She saw twenty years of friendship in that smile, but something else, too. Her breath caught and she saw Pete in a new light.

When had she had fallen in love with her best friend?

Chapter Two

Pete's phone rang at just past eight in the morning. He parked the golf cart he was lining up out front of his family's business and pulled his phone from the cargo pocket of his shorts. Ellen's picture popped up on his screen. He'd taken the photo himself, a quick snap of her at the wheel of the White Pine Island Ferry.

"House cat answering service," he said.

Ellen laughed on the other end of the call. "That's your worst one ever. No house cat would bother to answer the phone."

"That's why they need an answering service."

It was one of the things he'd miss. Making up a silly way to answer her phone calls and hearing her laugh. What would happen to their friendship if—when—he moved to the mainland?

"I need your help," Ellen said.

Pete felt a rush of adrenaline. Ellen never needed his help. She was the one who always had her life put together. Hell, she was the one coming to his rescue most of the time.

"Anything," he said.

"The hotel van is dead."

"And you want me to arrange a funeral?"

"Pete, I'm desperate. Our driver says it's some sensor in the ignition and we need a part from the dealership on the mainland. I guess it's happened before."

"I'm listening."

"The part will be available tomorrow, but in the mean time, we have dozens of guests arriving today for a fancy wedding tomorrow. They'll need a ride up to the hotel, and our twelve-seater golf carts are already being used for a recreation program this afternoon."

Pete glanced down the line of carts ready for the holiday crowds looking for a rental and a good time. He could spare a few for the Grand Hotel guests.

"Which ferry?" he asked.

"Mostly the two and four o'clock ones this afternoon. Maybe the six o'clock, but I doubt it. People will want to get here and unpack before the dinner hour."

"I'll have a fleet waiting at the dock," he said. "Maybe I'll even wear my Santa suit."

"Thanks. What would I do without you?" Ellen asked.

Guilt skewered his lungs. He was glad they were on the phone and he didn't have to face her right now. He had resolved to tell her last night, but he'd never worked up the courage. He had to tell her before she heard it from someone else—and on such a small island where everyone knew everyone else, he was running a hell of a risk that she'd find out McCormack Golf Cart Rentals was for sale.

"If I know you," Pete said, attempting a light tone, "you'd find a way. You could always invite me to the fancy wedding, especially if there's good food and an open bar."

Ellen groaned on her end of the phone line. "I'm expected to put on a dress and be helpful. The wedding is the daughter of a guest who's stayed here year after year. The beauty pageant type."

"Does she have a little dog in her purse?"

"Thank goodness we have a no pets policy at the Grand, so I don't know. Her name is Priscilla, and I think somehow her sister Bethany got all the nice genes in the family."

Pete dug in his pocket for golf cart keys while he talked with Ellen on the phone.

"Is this the Bethany your brother was grumbling about over a beer a few nights ago?"

"Probably. She's smart and pretty, but she's giving him all kinds of crap about his golf course."

"She doesn't like golf?"

Ellen laughed. "She doesn't like all the lawn chemicals it takes to maintain a golf course. She's some kind of environmental crusader. She may also hate golf, but that's not my problem. I've got a transportation nightmare. Can you imagine inviting over a hundred guests to your wedding on an island?"

"I don't think I know a hundred people," Pete said.

"I think it's crazy to have a princess wedding, but it's good business for the hotel. As long as they get on the ferry and I make sure they get up the hill to the hotel with all their matching luggage."

"You'll pull it off," Pete said, holding the phone to his ear with his shoulder while he turned the key and tested the lights on a golf cart.

"I already considered stealing the gardener's wheelbarrow and shoving people up the hill, but my parents have a certain expectation of classy behavior."

"The family curse," Pete said. "My parents…"

He almost told Ellen his parents were shopping for a senior living complex on the mainland and his future was open wider than the Milky Way. But now was not the time. Not when Ellen needed his help.

"What about your parents?" she prompted.

"They're happy if I tuck in my shirt and replace my sneakers at least once a year," he said.

"I love you, Pete. And your smelly old shoes."

Of course she did. She had for years. In the same way she loved sunshine, the island, and her brothers and sister. And she never wanted any of those things to change.

"Same to you, Els," he said. He slid his phone back in his pocket and mentally rearranged his plans for the day.

Pete crossed the wide gravel area where they parked the waiting golf carts. They owned four dozen carts, and because it was the only rental place on the island, most days all the carts saw some action. The new website Pete had created a year ago so patrons could reserve a cart ahead of time had made accounting for all the carts easier, and it also created a record of profitability which would help sell the place.

He shoved open the door of the office building. Basically a shed, the steel-sided structure had a sliding front window for interacting with customers, a desk, and a computer. In the past two years, Pete had added a radio, better lighting, a rolling chair, and electrical outlets. A calendar of pictures from White Pine Island hung on the wall, the December page a picture of the Grand Hotel decorated for Christmas.

The office was comfortable. Familiar. The only thing he could call his own. But it wasn't his own.

He opened a tab on the computer screen to view the daily reservations spreadsheet. Nearly half the fleet was reserved and paid for in advance today, but he could still spare a few for the Grand Hotel.

Pete's father, Marty McCormack, stuck his head in the front window. Cancer-free now for almost a year, the elder McCormack had filled out a little after the ravaging chemo treatments. His eyes were bright again, and he had a fresh crop of white hair.

"Did you see our ad?" Marty asked. He shoved a copy of the Oceanview newspaper across the counter. "I don't see how much good it will do because I doubt anyone over there is looking to move over here and take on this business, but your mother thought we should start local."

Pete picked up the paper which was folded to the classified ads section. *Thriving White Pine Island Business For Sale* the headline of the advertisement announced. Was their business thriving? He'd been so busy worrying about not letting his parents down as he'd built up their business over the past two years, he'd hardly stopped to consider the steady stream of profits. It would be a great investment for someone, especially with the capital improvements he'd made and the solid financial outlook it had now—thanks to him.

Pete skimmed the rest of the text which described the home, maintenance garage, rental office, and fleet of golf carts. He should have felt a huge sense of relief. The family albatross was being given permission to fly away. Pete could do anything he wanted now. He could move to the mainland and start his own electrical business, the thing he'd always said he wanted.

Instead of happiness at seeing the ad, though, he imagined Ellen's face if she happened to see it. He did not want her to pick up a copy of the paper, and he could only hope she was too busy with the impending wedding weekend to read the classified ads.

Thank goodness his parents hadn't placed an advertisement with the local weekly paper which was no more than a grapevine of island gossip published every Saturday.

"Comes out in the island paper tomorrow," Marty continued. "Just in case there's anyone crazy enough on this island to be interested."

Pete's heart sank. Either Ellen would see the ad which would be conspicuous in the tiny paper, or someone would surely tell her. He had only one more day of pretending things were still the same with his life and his best friend on White Pine Island.

****

Ellen rolled up to the ferry dock in the six-seater golf cart she'd forced her brother to give her for the day. His main goal in life was building up the reputation of the golf course, and he claimed he couldn't spare any carts to haul guests to "some damn wedding." Ellen had suspected his feelings about the sister of the bride had something to do with his attitude about helping, but she had reminded him that the Grand Hotel was their livelihood. And she also threatened to skewer him with a golf club if he didn't cooperate.

At least he'd let her have the largest cart from his precious stable. He'd also allowed her two four-seaters which she had conscripted bell hops into driving for the day.

When Ellen parked the cart, the two o'clock ferry was just a hundred yards offshore. Jimmy, her fellow captain and the only other person on the island with a license to pilot the ferry, was probably finishing his spiel welcoming guests to the year-round resort island.

Ellen stepped out of her cart and noticed the other two Grand Hotel carts were already waiting, their drivers standing ready. Instead of her usual captain's or pilot's uniform, Ellen had borrowed a bell hop uniform from the laundry at the hotel. She wore a white button-down shirt with GH embroidered on the chest pocket, burgundy pants, and a black and burgundy cap, also embroidered with a large gold GH. She had pinned on a black nametag with only her first name, no indication that she was the daughter of the owners.

"Nice disguise," a voice said from behind her. The sound of Pete's voice sent vibrations through her. She had lain awake all night revisiting the moment she realized her love for her lifelong friend was not the platonic love she'd enjoyed for almost twenty years. And now she had no idea what to do about it. Earlier in the morning, she'd ended their call by telling him she loved him. But they'd been saying that for years. Everyone on the island knew *that* they loved each other. But not *how* they loved each other. And neither had she...until last night.

When she turned around and saw him, would it be the good old Pete who had been her best friend all her life? Or would it be the man she suddenly saw in a different light who made her heart race and her stomach flutter?

She turned around, expecting to see Pete in his usual island apparel.

But he wasn't wearing worn cargo shorts and a t-shirt advertising his family business. Instead, he wore dark shorts with a neat crease, a crisp white polo, and a Santa hat. The shirt fit just snugly enough to highlight his broad chest. The shorts showed off his long legs. He wore boat shoes with no socks. Ellen kept her focus low for a moment. How did the man have such sexy ankles, for heaven's sake, and she'd never noticed?

"I like your disguise, too," she said, hoping to keep her voice level and light. "No one would know you were the heir to a golf cart empire in those playboy clothes."

"Ouch. I was hoping the hat took away from the men's catalog look."

"It does," she said, smiling. "But you still look nice. I'll bet all the women who come off the ferry will choose your golf cart over mine."

She would.

"And I'm sure all the men will pick you," he said.

What was that look on his face? She thought she knew every single expression Pete could muster. But this one looked almost…possessive. His eyes darkened as they flicked over her. That had never happened before. Had it?

She swallowed. Silence slipped between them as they stood near the sunny dock, but it was interrupted when the arriving ferry sounded its horn.

Ellen jumped. Pete reached out and placed a hand on her arm. He still had the new expression on his face. And now his hand was on her upper arm, heat from his fingers seeping into her skin. The shock of recognition that had whacked her in the head last night was even stronger today.

How was she going to get through a day of working alongside a man who suddenly made her want something she couldn't have?

It was out of the question. She could not risk her friendship by having these thoughts…or acting on these thoughts. Impossible. If she stepped into his arms and kissed him right now, he would either laugh—which would be horrifying, or run away—which would be devastating. She had made a similar mistake five years ago. Alex had been part of their circle before friendship turned into a brief summer romance. However, he left the island when the summer ended and his texts and calls got less and less frequent until he finally confessed to her that their fling didn't mean anything to him. It certainly hadn't meant he wanted to be tied down to the *little* island where he'd grown up.

For months she had wondered if she had driven him away. Had whined to Pete about the stupidity of ruining a friendship. Had vowed never to make such a painful mistake again. She'd kept that vow, and she had to continue keeping it.

Ellen turned, subtly extricating herself from Pete's touch.

"Here they come," she said.

Pete shaded his eyes and looked at the group disembarking. Ellen did the same, and she divided the group mentally. Some of them were day tourists wearing shorts and flip flops. They headed for downtown, and many of them would probably stop and check out a rental golf cart. They'd eat at the island restaurants, drink at the bars, risk a sunburn on the beaches, and have some reckless fun away from their cares on the mainland.

But the other half of the new arrivals wore resort wear. Men with linen shirts tucked in. Belts and dress shoes. Women with floral shirts matching their Capri pants and summery blazers.

"I'll bet there's at least one dog in a purse in that group," Pete observed.

"Better not be. If there is, it'll have to bunk with you."

"Edison prefers his solitude," Pete said. "And he's never shared his bed, that I know of."

Ellen wished Pete wouldn't talk about sharing beds. She was trying hard not to imagine what it would be like to be wrapped in his arms. In his bed. She'd seen his bare chest many times as they'd grown up swimming and playing on the island. She'd seen his bedroom many times as they'd shared pizza, played cards, and talked about everything. He'd often been eager to show her his electrical experiments which he hid in his room so his mother wouldn't freak out about him playing with amps and voltage. She smiled remembering the hole he'd burned in the carpet and how she'd helped him move his bed to cover it.

She thought she knew everything about Pete and her feelings for him.

Why was her heart betraying her like this?

The wave of people lugging rolling suitcases got closer, and Ellen started to believe she was going to have to make several trips, leaving hotel guests waiting.

"My dad's on his way with one of our other six-seaters," Pete said.

"You're a lifesaver. I was just starting to panic."

"I know," Pete said. "The vein on your temple was jumping like it does when you're mad or upset."

Ellen touched the vein next to her right eye. It was throbbing. But it wasn't just the stupid golf carts and wedding guests. Pete, with his observant ways and his genuine caring for her, was going to cause her a stroke. She tried to think of something immensely unpleasant or unflattering about him.

She thought of the shockingly white tuxedo he rented for their high school prom. A pathetically small prom hosted in the ballroom at her family's hotel. The dozen or so seniors and juniors with a smattering of underclassmen or guests from the mainland had enjoyed a fancy dinner in formal attire before moving on to trying not to touch each other on the dance floor. It was practically incest, dancing with people she'd known all her life. Yes, the tuxedo was a failure, but she and Pete had still stayed up all night talking. *Not working.*

"You can't make it stop by keeping your finger on it," Pete said, gesturing toward the pulsing vein in her temple. "You need happy thoughts. For example, a dog could escape a purse and cause havoc at the wedding."

"There will be no dogs in purses."

"So you think," he said.

Ellen sighed. "I can't punch someone wearing a Santa hat. It violates the spirit of the holidays."

Pete smiled. "I'll shut up and drive."

"But be charming to my guests."

"Still hoping for an invite to the open bar reception," he said.

"Why don't you come by later like you usually do? I could text you when they cut the cake and I'll meet you on the porch with cake and champagne."

"Just one of the many benefits of being best friends with the island hotel princess," Pete said.

"If I were a princess, I'd have my footmen deliver your cake."

"Ah, but then you'd miss the pleasure of seeing me."

Ellen laughed. "I would."

Was this flirting? It sounded like flirting. She did not flirt, as a general rule. And especially not with the one person on earth who could break her heart if she let him.

Chapter Three

After shuttling Grand Hotel guests up the hill all day, Pete needed a drink. There was nothing wrong with his passengers. Sure, they were a little overdressed with expensive luggage and more perfume than necessary, but they were jovial. Excited for a holiday wedding at an exclusive resort, who wouldn't be? It wasn't the people he'd politely driven up to the hotel, it was his co-shuttler.

How was it possible Ellen could be sexy in a bell hop uniform? A button-down shirt and burgundy pants should not be attractive on anyone.

But it was. And Pete had battled heat all day. Heat, and inappropriate feelings for his best friend. Even if he could consider crossing the friend line, even if she would be interested in dancing that dance…now was not the time. Not now when his life was at a crossroads.

His phone rang as he drove down the hill from the hotel on his last run. It was nearly dinner time on Friday afternoon. Fortunately, his mom had managed the golf cart business while he and his dad were shuttling hotel guests. He knew from past experience that a generous check from the hotel would arrive at his parents' business by the end of the week, and it would more than cover the cost of cart rental and their time.

He glanced at the unfamiliar number on his phone as he kept one hand on the wheel. He swiped the screen and said hello.

"Pete McCormack?"

"Speaking."

"This is Chris Garvey from Oceanview Electric."

Pete pulled off the narrow road and parked under a shade tree, his senses on alert.

"We got your resume and wanted to talk with you about possibly joining our team of electricians."

"That's great," Pete said, his voice sounding unnatural to him. "I'd love to meet with you."

"I see you live on White Pine Island," Chris said. "I'll be upfront with you. One of the things we'll talk about in the interview is location."

Ellen drove by on her golf cart. She had three passengers and a load of luggage. She gave him a curious look at she passed him and waved. *No doubt she's wondering why I pulled off the road to talk on my cell phone.*

Pete waved and tried to force a smile for Ellen.

"I understand relocation would be necessary," he said.

"Can you come in a day next week and talk with me and my partner?"

"Any day," Pete said.

"I'll call you Monday and we'll set up a time. We'll work it in around projects before we take time off for the holidays."

Pete slipped the phone back in the pocket of his shorts after they ended the call. From his shady spot on the hill, he could see the entire downtown area of White Pine Island. It shimmered in the afternoon sunlight. The bars and restaurants were inviting and would be busy on a Friday night in holiday party season.

The island was the only home he'd ever known. He glanced across the Atlantic Ocean. Barely visible in the distance was the mainland. Only one or two buildings caught the light and suggested civilization over there. But there was a whole world waiting for him, a world he'd always thought he wanted to be part of but had delayed because of his father's illness.

And now? It was now or never. Getting his degree took a lot of work and it was his passion, figuring out wiring schematics, electricity running through wires and switches.

He pulled back onto the road, putting the Grand Hotel farther behind him as he drove toward town. Instead of checking in at McCormack Rentals, he drove straight to his friend's bar and restaurant one street back from the water's edge downtown. Because of its location and low key signage out front, the bar was mostly known to the locals. With dark wood paneling and booths, it was a haven from sun and tourists.

"Don't marry a girl from the mainland," Chuck said as soon as Pete grabbed a bar stool.

Without asking, Chuck filled a draft beer glass with Pete's favorite and slid it to him. Pete took a drink and waited while his friend took an order from a patron down the bar. He knew what was coming. A few years ago, Chuck had married a tourist. Pete was his best man, and two other guys they went to high school with rounded out the male half of the bridal party. The wedding had taken place in the gazebo by the waterfront downtown on a sunny summer day.

The bride, Mainland Marian they called her, brought a pack of strangers for her half of the wedding party. No surprise, of course she would bring her friends and family from Oceanview. The wedding seemed like a fairy tale at the time, although Pete remembered Ellen's narrowed eyes during the fancy affair. He'd jokingly asked her if she was jealous and she'd crossed her arms and glared at him. Over a drink at the reception, she'd made her position clear. The wedding wouldn't work out. Mainland people don't understand life on the island. Not three-hundred-and-sixty-five days a year life anyway.

It was one of Ellen's hang-ups—being overly protective of their fellow island residents and a total bulldog when it came to the merits of island vs. mainland life. Not that she knew or ever wanted to find out what it was like to live across the water. She considered it tragic that her poor sister Kate had been dragged "over there" by her marriage a few years back.

"What's up with Mainland Marian?" Pete asked when Chuck wiped down the bar in his direction.

"Christmas shopping. Again."

"Christmas is only eleven days away," Pete said.

"I know. Believe me. She's made three trips on the ferry already. Plus, she wants to spend Christmas Eve and Christmas Day on the mainland with her family."

"Did you try inviting them here?"

"Tried. But, as she pointed out, we've spent all three holidays of our married life on the island."

"Split the difference?" Pete asked.

"No ferries on Christmas," Chuck said.

"Forgot about that," Pete said. He'd never spent the holidays on the mainland. Even though his older sister moved to Oceanview five years ago, she'd come home for Christmas every year. It would be strange to have to compromise and divide up the time. Maybe it was a good thing he was considering moving to the mainland when his parents did. It would be simpler.

But when would he give Ellen her Christmas present? And would he still be invited to the annual party for locals at the Grand Hotel?

"Maybe I could ask Ellen to fly us over on Christmas Day in time for dinner," Chuck said, pausing in his circular pattern wiping down the bar.

A sliver of jealousy hit Pete. He usually got together with Ellen and exchanged gifts at some point on Christmas day. It gave them both an excuse to escape their families for a few minutes. Would this be his last Christmas slipping away with Ellen and sitting by the lake or riding bikes around the quiet island on the holiday?

"I'm thinking of moving to the other side," Pete said suddenly. He had to talk about it with someone.

"Wondered," Chuck said. He leaned his broad forearms on the bar and gave Pete his attention. When Pete's classmate had bought the downtown bar, no one was surprised. Chuck had long been known as "the listener." One of those people who was capable of hearing an entire story without commenting, he was also known as "the vault." Running a bar and lending an ear was the perfect occupation for the affable giant.

"Did you hear the business is up for sale?"

Chuck nodded.

"My parents want to move into some kind of low-maintenance senior living in Oceanview. They'll be closer to my sister and medical care."

"Your dad's better, isn't he?"

"He is. But they're not getting any younger."

Chuck filled a basket with nuts and pretzels and set it between them.

"So this is your big chance to play with electricity and have your own life," he said. "What are you going to do?"

Pete scooped up a handful of salty snacks. "With the business being sold, there's nothing keeping me here on the island."

"Nothing?" Chuck asked. He raised an eyebrow, but moved on down the bar, not forcing Pete to answer the question he needed to answer most.

****

Saturday, December 15, was a beautiful day for a wedding. Blue skies, some tiny fluffy clouds, and warm temperatures typical of the warm winter off the Georgia coast. A very slight breeze wouldn't ruffle the bride's perfect hair or dress much, Ellen thought as she taxied in to land at the tiny island airport.

If her plane didn't smell like a funeral parlor, it would also be nice. She'd made the early morning flight to the mainland for the buckets and bouquets of wedding flowers. There was nothing unusual about being sent on the flower run. To keep fresh greenhouse flowers at the reception desk and on the parlor and dining room tables, she made at least one trip a week all year long. She liked the smell of roses and she'd learned to tolerate carnations. Daisies were her favorite with their non-fussy aroma. Ellen's mother usually took her feelings into account when she ordered the weekly flowers.

However, the bride ruled the floral order today, and Ellen's plane was ready to vomit orchids and peonies. If she could have opened a window for fresh air as she crossed the stretch of Atlantic Ocean, she would have. Thank goodness the hotel van was back in service and would meet her at the airstrip to unload the fifteen dozen fussy flowers.

"It'll take me a week to get the smell out of my plane," she complained to Yauncey, the hotel's van driver.

"Unroll the windows and leave it in the sun," he advised. "If that doesn't work, you could put a box of baking soda under the seat."

He leaned in and started lifting the buckets of flowers. "Maybe a box under each one of the seats," he amended after he got a whiff of the plane's interior.

"Weddings," Ellen grumbled. "I usually only like the fancy food and the cake. Especially the cake."

Yauncey climbed into the plane and handed a box of boutonnieres and corsages to Ellen. "This one should have some excitement to it, I think," he said. "The family has stayed here often enough, they…uh…feel invested in the Grand Hotel."

Ellen laughed. "You mean they think they own it."

"I wouldn't have put it that way since I just work here."

"Priscilla has been a thorn in my side every year when they visit. I know she thinks I'm just some hired hand who runs the ferry and the plane."

"You could show up at her reception looking prettier than she does," Yauncey suggested. "I could make you a crown out of aluminum foil."

"I'm not getting in a contest with a beauty queen. Besides, it's her day. She should be the prettiest. I think I'll stay in the background," she said. She winked at her old friend Yauncey. "After I get a piece of cake."

Relieved of the powerfully aromatic flowers, Ellen checked in with the small office at the island airport before she walked the short distance down the hill to her little house. The island airport was at the highest elevation and her house was on the way down to the bluff where the Grand Hotel perched.

Alone at her house, Ellen shoved hangers around in her closet while she considered her evening attire. She'd been to weddings at the hotel before, acting informally as a hostess or representative of the hotel. Such hostess duties meant she was on hand to run errands and smooth over problems. One time, she had flown a runaway bride back to the mainland just before she was supposed to walk down the improvised aisle in the garden.

She doubted that would be happening today. Priscilla was fully in command of herself, her groom, and her future plans. Perhaps her younger sister Bethany might like to tip back a bottle of wine in a quiet corner of the lobby with Ellen, but Priscilla would be firmly in the spotlight.

Ellen had no plans to be in the spotlight, but she still had to choose something suitable to wear. And by suitable, she meant something that her mother would like. She'd already seen her mother's dress for tonight. It was a knee length evergreen sheath dress with a matching jacket. The jacket had a few sequins and a lace panel. It said "holiday elegance" without saying "I'm with the bride's family."

Her father would be in his usual black tuxedo. Men had it easy.

Lucky Pete. He didn't even have to dress up. She'd asked him to stop by halfway through the reception, and they'd find some empty rocking chairs on the porch to eat cake and have a drink. It was the least she could do to express her thanks for his chauffeur services. It wasn't all that unusual. Right? She'd saved him wedding cake countless times.

This is not new.

Ellen pulled out three cocktail dresses. Her favorite navy blue one that made her eyes look more blue. A burgundy one she could only pull off if she had an even tan. And a black one with a full lace overlay. Very feminine. Very mother-approved. But also very curve-hugging.

Pete had never seen her in the black dress. But he would tonight. She was playing with fire, trying to see if the newly-discovered flames were only on her side, in her mind.

She put the dress and a pair of black heels in a garment bag and trekked down the hill to the rear entrance of the hotel.

"Thank goodness you're here," the front desk manager said. "The bride's grandmother surprised her by flying in from Europe."

"Quite a surprise," Ellen commented.

"And the old gal's waiting at the airport in Savannah."

"Geez."

"Ellen!" her father exclaimed. Edward Phillips emerged from his office, his dark suit and darker frown making Ellen wonder if they should take the "destination wedding" package off their website.

"I hope you feel like flying," he said, giving his daughter a quick embrace. "We have three hours until the garden ceremony. Can you make it to Savannah and back?"

Ellen smiled. "All I need is a ride to the airport and five boxes of baking soda."

By the time Ellen made the round trip to pick up the surprise guest, she barely had time to shimmy into the dress, brush her hair, apply lipstick, and slide into the high heels. She stood off to the side, watching the bride and her party process down an aisle in the garden constructed of white chairs, a trellis, and dozens of flowers.

Ellen's first cousin Samantha grinned at her as they both waited for the long gushy vows to conclude. Samantha was the closest thing to a sister Ellen had now that Kate had moved to the mainland. Sam's father Charles and Ellen's father Ed shared joint ownership of the hotel, as the cousins would someday. Samantha possessed the hospitality gene in the form of decorating, arranging flowers, and being charming to people. Even though they had different talents, and Ellen thought Samantha with her long red hair was ten times prettier, they had always gotten along. The only real test of their friendship was several years ago when Samantha had talked Ellen into going out with Alex. In her defense, she couldn't have known he would leave the island and never look back.

When the late afternoon wedding finished, the reception in the ballroom began. Ellen and Samantha helped usher the guests into the ballroom where an imposing white cake presided over an elaborately decorated table.

Cake. Her reason for loving weddings. When she saw the monstrous cake, she was glad she'd invited Pete. No one would notice or care if she grabbed a few slices and met her best friend on the porch.

Ellen attempted to blend in with the servers and hotel staff while the usual wedding reception formalities went off in excruciating perfection. Toasts. Ceremonial dances. Pictures. Would they ever cut that cake? And where was the drama? *Sigh.* Of course Priscilla would have a perfect wedding where no one got drunk and said something inappropriate or pulled off an unforgettable dance destined to become a viral video.

It was dull, but it would make lovely pictures in a magazine.

Everyone was dancing now under holiday lights strung across the ballroom. White peonies, red ribbons, and candles decorated the tables. The bride had to be delighted, no matter how high her expectations were. From her position in the semi-darkness at a back wall, Ellen enjoyed the scene, watching the dancers. Her brother Ned was on the dance floor with Bethany, the sister of the bride. A bridesmaid, not a maid of honor. There had to be a story there, but the story of why she was dancing so closely with Ellen's brother seemed a lot more interesting at the moment. If she didn't know better, Ellen would think they were in love.

She had to admire the way Ned took his work seriously. If winning over an environmental crusader who was making things difficult for his precious golf course meant dancing with her, he was taking one for the team right now.

Her eyes cut to the ballroom entrance. Was Pete waiting for her text? Was he already on the porch? She wished she could dance with him. Could feel his arms around her, his cheek brushing hers. Her chest fluttered at the thought.

And it was the fluttering that was so dangerous. She'd always looked forward to seeing him, but a new awareness had rushed over her two nights ago. She was out of her mind, and the only thing that would save her was if Pete didn't feel the same way about her. It took a match and a strike to make a flame, didn't it?

Finally. Ellen sent Pete a quick message as the bride and groom smiled sweetly for the cameras and cut the cake. Hotel staff moved in quickly to plate and serve the gorgeous confection. And Ellen grabbed two slices and slipped out the rear exit of the ballroom. In her high heels, she carefully navigated the flagstone walkway leading to the porch while she balanced the two white plates. She took her eyes off her feet for only a moment and looked up.

Pete stood on the edge of the porch, his face lost in shadow. He was waiting for her, just as he had before, many times. But suddenly it all felt new. Was it her feelings coloring everything she saw, or was there something about him tonight that told her for certain she was in deep trouble?

Chapter Four

Pete drew in a steadying breath when he saw Ellen approaching in a body-hugging dress. Her long blonde hair flowed over her shoulders. It was almost completely dark as the calendar ticked toward the shortest day of the year, but his best friend was illuminated by Christmas lights as she picked her way along the path toward him. And he would know her anywhere, just from her walk, her presence, everything about her.

It was worse than he thought, the strength of his feelings for her. But a relationship with Ellen Phillips was just one more missed chance in his life. Even as he considered taking a chance and grabbing his future with both hands, he was painfully conscious of what he was leaving behind.

"I hope you haven't been waiting long," Ellen said.

"Only a few minutes." *Years, ever since I realized how beautiful you are and how right the world feels when you're next to me.*

"Check these out," she said, holding up the cake slices as she climbed the steps to the porch. "It was the fanciest cake I've ever seen. These better taste as good as they look."

She set the plates on a little table between two rocking chairs. "Be right back," she said. "Have to grab something to wash this down."

"Need help?"

She had already turned away, but she swung around and smiled at him, her face catching the glow from the Christmas lights. He was the one who needed help.

"Wait right here for me," she said.

Pete sat and rocked while he waited for Ellen to return. He had to tell her tonight. It was a miracle she didn't already know. And he knew she didn't. It would have shown on her face. Neither of them was any good at hiding things from the other one.

They'd eat the cake first. Have a drink. And then he would tell her he was leaving White Pine Island.

He heard her heels clicking on the porch floor before he saw her. He got up and took both very full glasses of champagne.

"Only spilled a little," she said.

She sipped her drink and set it on the table. Picked up the cake plate and lopped off a huge piece with the heavy silver fork.

"The chocolate looked good, but I knew you liked white," she said. "The beer selection also looked good, but I know your dirty little secret. Golf cart mechanic with a hidden passion for bubbly."

"You'll ruin my reputation as a man's man," Pete said.

"Your reputation is safe."

Ellen kicked off her shoes. How many times had they sat, barefoot, on this porch? Or on the dock downtown. Or on the patio at his parents' house behind the golf cart rental. Or on the beaches that surround the island.

Pete finished his cake and drank half his champagne. It was comfortable, sitting on the porch of the

Grand Hotel with someone who knew him as well as he knew himself. But he had to tell her.

"You might as well say it," she said. She put down her empty plate and sipped her drink. "I know whatever is bothering you is something big. And I suspect I'm not going to like it."

"My parents are selling their business," he said. Might as well go big.

"Oh," she said. She put down her glass and sat back in the big rocking chair.

"They want to retire and move to the mainland where they'll be closer to my sister. Closer to healthcare."

Ellen didn't say anything. He knew she was a good listener, she always let him finish without interrupting. But tonight he almost wished she would stop him before he said one of the hardest things in the world.

"This means I don't have to run the family business anymore."

Ellen picked up her glass, took a slow sip, and put it back on the table.

"It means I can finally use my degree. Strike out on my own."

Why doesn't she say something? Her face was shadowed when she leaned back in the chair.

"Ellen, I'm thinking..."

She leaned forward suddenly and he saw her expression in the glow of the holiday lights. Her eyes glistened. "Of leaving the island," she said.

He nodded. It was too painful to speak.

Ellen jumped up, sending her chair rocking. Pete got up, ready to stop her if she planned to run before she listened to his explanation.

But she didn't run. She put her arms around his waist and held him so tight he couldn't move. The top of her head was just below his chin. He slid his arms around her and held her, wishing the moment would never end. Of all the reactions he'd expected, this one surprised him. He'd thought she might smile and tough it out, supporting him even if she didn't want him to go. He'd considered the possibility of her punching him in the gut and telling him he wasn't allowed to leave.

But this silence, her arms and scent wrapped around him, was unexpected. And wonderful. Was it possible...was it? Did she feel something beyond a lifetime of friendship for him?

And what should he do now?

****

Ellen's cheek was pressed to Pete's hard chest. She knew the t-shirt he was wearing, knew all the clothes in his wardrobe. Had memorized his scent of Dial soap and pine trees. But she'd never clung to him like this before. Had never let raw feelings drive her actions.

He couldn't leave. Tears stung her eyes and threatened to betray her by dampening his shirt. Just when she had finally realized her feelings for him were far beyond friendship, he was leaving. She squeezed her eyes shut and forced herself to confront the truth. Had she known he was thinking of leaving? Is that why she had the revelation?

She drew in a ragged breath. No. The feelings had been there for…how long? But now what? Grabbing Pete in a bear hug was the only thing she could think of to do instead of breaking down in a sobbing puddle.

But when he slid his arms around her and rested his chin on the top of her head, and she heard his heart racing through the solid wall of his chest, she knew this was more than two friends saying goodbye. For both of them.

How long had he known?

She couldn't think of what to say. She could only think of what to do. She tipped her head back, raised up on her bare toes, and kissed him. Her kiss was a mere brush of lips at first. A test. His lips responded to hers and deepened the kiss.

Was it possible? And, sweet sunshine, was it amazing. Her body lit up like a holiday candle.

His hand cradled the back of her head, holding her so his lips could encompass hers. She slid her tongue into his mouth and felt him groan.

There were years of kisses in that one.

She was kissing her best friend in a dark corner of her porch at her family's hotel. She was kissing her best friend. And nothing had ever felt so right. His lips fit hers, his arms and the quiet energy she'd always associated with his love for electricity surrounded her. She wanted to fall into Pete and never climb out.

Floorboards creaked. She heard footsteps and quiet conversation as someone passed by them on the porch. Before she drew any more attention to herself, she should probably find a more secluded place. *Like one of the eighty hotel rooms only steps away.* She broke the kiss and pulled back just enough to see his face.

"Why didn't we do that years ago?" he asked. He was breathing fast and his voice sounded strange.

"Can I blame the champagne and wedding cake?" she asked.

Pete laughed. A laugh she'd heard a thousand times. But it was different when she was so close to him her hair fell over his shoulder.

"I hope you're not thinking it was a mistake to kiss me like that," he said. "Because it didn't feel like it to me."

Ellen swallowed. It *was* a mistake. A huge one. She would never have been okay with Pete leaving White Pine Island before. And now she sure as hell wouldn't. She'd just made everything ten times harder.

"It was just a kiss," she said. "A goodbye kiss. Since you're thinking of leaving and all."

Pete cocked his head slightly and his eyes bored into hers. "Are you telling me that was only because I'm leaving?"

"Of course it was. Have I ever done that before?"

"No. I would've remembered."

"So there you have it. And I should get back to the reception just in case they need me." She tried to step backward, but his arms held her.

"We're not going to talk about this?"

Her heart raced. She couldn't talk about that kiss. Talking about it would make her want to do it again. And it was one of the bravest and most dangerous things she'd ever done. Braver than becoming a boat captain. Gutsier than flying a plane alone for the first time. And yet absolutely stupid.

"Sure we can talk," she said. "So, tell me about your plans on the mainland. Got a job lined up? Bought your own car yet? Need help picking out furniture for your new place?"

"That's not what I mean and you know it."

Fresh tears stung her eyes at his tone. She couldn't fight with Pete. They had never even argued. Why should they have? He was her rock. She was his. But the rock was crumbling. She shook her head instead of answering, not trusting her voice.

"We'll talk tomorrow," he said. He released her and smoothed a hand over her hair. The gesture was full of affection.

And regret?

He stooped, picked up her shoes, and handed them to her.

"Don't go back to the reception tonight," he said. "I know all the fun is gone for you when the cake has been served."

Their empty cake plates mocked them from the table between the two empty chairs.

"Do you need a ride home?" she asked.

He shook his head. "Brought my own cart."

At the mention of the golf cart, reality slapped her again. No more golf cart rental business for Pete's family. No more McCormack family on the island. No more Pete.

She hated change. Feared change. Why couldn't her fairy tale life stay exactly as it was?

"Do you want me to take you home?" he asked.

She shook her head, never taking her eyes off his.

If it were another night, Pete would drive her home without even asking, but something had taken their usual pattern and twisted it into a knot.

"Goodnight Els," he said. Pete turned and disappeared into the darkness.

No casual "love you," which was their usual farewell. Clearly their love was no longer casual. And their friendship was no longer easy.

Ellen wanted to run after him and beg him not to leave. But her heart was already out on a cliff, in grave danger of falling and breaking into irreparable pieces.

****

Pete pulled up to Ellen's cottage before seven the next morning. He grabbed his toolbox and got out of his golf cart. Tall enough not to need a ladder, he examined the broken light on her front porch. Unscrewed the bottom plate. And discovered some island creature had chewed through the wires. He dug through the toolbox and pulled out electrical tape. A temporary fix until he could run some new wires.

He thought he wasn't making any noise, but the front door swung open and Ellen stood there in blue and white striped pajamas. She didn't look angry, he noted. It had been a bold move showing up here this early the morning after they took the rules of friendship and rewrote them.

But he had to, today of all days.

"I could flip the porch light switch on and kill you right now," she said, a small smile quirking her lips.

"Happy Birthday, Ellen," he said pleasantly. "My life is in your hands."

Her smile faded and she studied his face. If his life truly were in her hands, he would feel safe. And happy.

She gestured toward the dismantled light fixture. "This better not be my present."

Pete laughed. "I can do better than that."

She leaned against the doorframe and her smile returned. "You always do. Every single year."

The way she stood there and uttered the simple sentence felt like an invitation. Pete tossed the roll of black electrical tape onto the porch floor and crossed the narrow boards in two steps. He had to be closer to her.

"It's your birthday, so you can throw me out right now if you want to," he said.

"I can't throw you out if I haven't even asked you in yet."

"Do you want your present?"

Her grin widened. "Come in."

Pete held up one finger and returned to his cart where he retrieved a wrapped box.

"You never forget my birthday, even when everyone else loses track of it in the holiday rush."

He handed her the box. "And I never give you the old this is your Christmas and birthday gift combined line."

"You know I hate that."

"I know."

He couldn't take his eyes off her. Her hair was disheveled and there was a pillow line on her cheek. Her bare toes stuck out the bottom of the pajamas and he thought about all the skin between her head and her toes.

Pete cleared his throat. "I hope you'll like it."

Ellen turned and headed for the couch. Pete closed the door and followed. She sat crossed-legged with the gift on her lap.

"Open it," he said.

She tore off the paper, opened the flap on the black box inside, and lifted out a pair of expensive sunglasses.

Her smile started with her lips and encompassed her entire face. "I love it," she said, slipping the glasses on. She jumped up and dashed to the mirror hanging near the front door.

"I got the special glare resistant coating so you can fly with them and pilot the ferry," he said as he followed her to the mirror. "When you sat on your other ones at Chuck's bar last week, it was just the idea I needed."

"I hated those sunglasses anyway," she said. "But I love these already. And I love that you noticed I squashed my other pair."

She hugged Pete. The kind of hug he usually got when he gave her just the right thing for her birthday and then a just-right Christmas gift a week later. Every year.

He wasn't sure what to do. Should he give her the quick friendly hug he usually returned? Last night's clench and kiss was firmly on his mind and had been all through the dark hours of the night when he'd hardly slept.

He didn't have to make the decision. Ellen pulled back. Took off the sunglasses and laid them gently on the hall table. She looked him in the eye, a serious expression on her face.

"I haven't forgotten last night either," she said. "I know you're wondering whether you should give me the big brother hug and bum a sandwich from my kitchen. Or if we should do…uh…something else."

"We've never done…uh…something else."

"Do you want to do something else?"

Pete swiped a hand over his face. What was the right answer? The truth? The truth was hell, yes he did. Ellen was a sexy attractive woman he'd known and loved as long as he could remember. But he also knew it was a road that only ran one direction and there would be no returning if he went too far.

"Why did you kiss me last night?" he asked.

Ellen bit her lip. "It was the only thing I could think of to do."

"Because I'm talking about leaving."

"Not only because of that."

"Then why?" *Please tell me it's not only because things are changing. Because I've felt this way for a long time.*

"Because of the way I feel about you," she said. She looked down at her feet. "I'm twenty-five years old today. And I woke up this morning knowing something I never realized before."

"I hope you didn't find a wrinkle or a wart or something," he said. It was the kind of thing he'd say to his best friend, whether or not he wanted to scoop her up and take her into the bedroom where he knew the comforter was purple and the sheets were probably still warm and rumpled.

"I'm trying to be serious here, Pete."

He let out a long breath. "Me, too. But I'm scared to death right now. You've always been the brave one, flying planes and such."

"I should make this easy for you then," she said. "I woke up wishing you were next to me in my bed."

He swallowed. "I can make that happen."

She took his hand and held it between hers for a moment before she looked him in the eye. "Even though I've loved you since forever, I want you to know that crossing that line would be the bravest thing I've ever done."

"I'm willing," Pete said. His heart hammered. They were at a crossroads at the same time he was at a crossroads. Why did everything suddenly have to be so complicated? Only one thing was clear. He knew he wanted what Ellen was offering.

"I have to be at the ferry dock in less than an hour," Ellen said. "But Jimmy is taking over the ferry after I make the two o'clock run. That means I'll be free to go have fun later."

Fun was exactly what Pete had in mind. All kinds of fun. He ran the possibilities through his head, but he kept coming back to the bedroom only a dozen steps away.

"If someone asks me," Ellen said. She dipped her head and looked up at him, vulnerability etched on her face.

"I'll pick you up," he said, pulling her into his arms. "Prepare to have the best birthday you've ever had."

Chapter Five

"Maybe this can work," Ellen said to herself as she handed off the paperwork and the responsibility of running the island ferry to her partner. True to his word, Pete waited for her on the dock with a golf cart.

Ellen swung off the ferry, feeling lightness in every step. She took off her captain's hat and freed her hair from the band holding it back. Stripped off her captain's shirt to reveal a Grand Hotel t-shirt underneath with the signature logo of a green pine tree and a gold GH.

Pete stepped out of the golf cart. "If you're going to strip on the dock, I'm going to have to fight off other men," he said.

Ellen grinned, wadded up her shirt and hat and stowed them on the back seat of the golf cart. She noticed a blanket and several bags were already on the seat. "I don't want other men," she said. "I chose you to spend the day with."

They sat next to each other on the white vinyl seat.

"Do I kiss you?" Pete asked.

"I'm still getting used to the idea," Ellen said. *Certainly he could hear her heart thudding with anticipation.*

"Is that a yes?"

She kissed him on the lips, a quick kiss that promised more to come. Pete cleared his throat and put on his sunglasses. Although they'd known each other forever, this felt like a first date. As if they were treading carefully on sacred ground.

"We've got several hours of daylight left," he said. "I have a rough plan."

"Unless it requires special clothing, you can surprise me."

Pete took off his sunglasses and turned to her. His eyes were like green fire and she'd never seen him look more serious. "It does not require clothing," he said. And then he laughed and peeled out of the ferry parking lot.

With one hand draped over the top of the wheel, he drove them to a beach on the south side of the island that only the locals usually visited. They called it the "secret beach" because it had escaped being on the tourists' radar, but it wasn't necessarily a secret. It was just off the beaten path.

"Hungry?" Pete asked as he parked under a tree.

"Did you bring birthday cake?"

"No, but I brought your favorite chips and cookies from the market downtown. And cream soda."

"A man after my heart," she said.

"Of course I am." He stroked her cheek with two fingers. "I'd like to think I may already have it."

You certainly do, Ellen thought. *But where do we go from here?* Instead of speaking, she put her hand on his leg and gave his thigh a gentle squeeze. He slipped an arm around her and pulled her close. He kissed her neck and followed her jaw line to her lips.

"Can you believe I've never made out in a golf cart before?" he murmured.

Ellen pulled back and smiled. "We have a whole beach waiting for us."

She kicked off her shoes and left them in the golf cart. Pete did the same and they crossed the white sand, hand in hand. They sat on a log by the ocean and Pete handed out snacks from the grocery bag.

Ellen balanced her can of soda on her knee. "Do you think this could work?" she asked.

Pete let out a long breath. "You mean us being more than friends?"

"Yes."

"I hope so. Because if I have to go back to just friend status, it'll take me a long time to forget the way you kiss."

Ellen leaned closer and kissed him, a deep soft kiss that lasted long enough for a dozen waves to crash onto the shore near them.

"You mean like that?"

"Exactly like that."

"I never thought I could date someone from the island again after, you know," she said.

Pete nodded. "I know."

"Not that I had a plan or anything," Ellen said. "Maybe I was hoping my dream man would show up on my plane or at the hotel and pledge to stay forever on White Pine Island."

That used to be a requirement, one that had been reinforced when Alex left and never came back. In her dreams, she had never imagined dating someone who was not a permanent resident. But she was starting to get very lonely sticking to such a rigid set of rules.

She looked across the ocean. From the south side of the island, only a sliver of the mainland was visible. It was almost as if the island was all alone in a wide blue sea.

"The mainland always seems so far away," she said, "but I cross over in the ferry several times a day and fly there at least two or three times a week. Maybe it's not so far."

"It's not," Pete agreed.

Ellen turned her attention away from the water and looked at Pete. "Do you have to leave?" she asked. She had to ask. Had to give him a chance to talk it through. That's what a good friend would do, even if it broke her heart talking about it.

"That's a question I've been asking myself," he admitted.

"I don't want you to."

She shouldn't be doing this. Should not be interfering with his dreams and asking him to make a choice. It wasn't fair. What if the tables were turned? But they would never be. She would never leave the island. Her past was here, but more importantly, her future was here.

Where was Pete's future?

"My parents have worked hard for a long time," he said pensively, almost as if he was talking to himself. "I understand their decision. What my father went through…it was terrible."

"It makes you think about your life," Ellen agreed. She had been there with Pete through some dark times when they found out about his father's lymphoma. And then when they feared it had spread. She'd held his hand at the hospital. Hugged him. Told him she loved him and was there for him. She'd packed up five course dinners from the hotel and delivered them to Pete's family home behind the rental business. Had coaxed a smile out of his father by bringing him three different desserts to choose from. Had washed the dishes herself in the McCormack kitchen so Pete's mother wouldn't have to.

And she had celebrated with Pete's family when his father was declared cancer free. Had brought a bottle of champagne and cried happy tears with them. Surely she had known then that her relationship with Pete transcended friendship. She'd been a member of his family for years. Had it taken his potential leaving to jolt her into reality?

"And it makes sense for them to retire," Pete continued, interrupting her thoughts. "They have to sell the business and use the assets from it to buy a house. They're excited about it, even put an ad in the paper. I'm surprised you didn't see it."

Ellen shook her head. "Too busy with that red carpet wedding. I was blinded by all the jewelry."

"My sister in Oceanview will take care of them, and now that she's married, there will be grandkids." He smiled at Ellen. "You know my mother, she couldn't be four miles across the water from grandchildren."

"She'll want to cook for them," Ellen said, grinning.

Pete laughed. "Poor kids." He slid an arm around Ellen. He kissed her neck and lingered, his breath on her ear and her cheek.

"We've been to this beach a hundred times," he said. "Played Frisbee, swam, made campfires, drank underage a few times."

His lips touched her ear as he spoke and sent vibrations throughout her body.

"There's something we've never done," she whispered. Something she had only done with one other person. And that person had left and broken her heart. But Pete was different. What they had meant more. She knew it. And even though her fragile grasp on a world she wanted to keep exactly as it was seemed to be slipping, there was something she had to give Pete. And take from him.

She got up and grabbed the blanket from the back seat of the golf cart. Flipping it in the air, she spread it on the sand where they would be sheltered by some trees. She stepped on to the blanket and sat down, holding out her hand as an invitation. Pete joined her, moving slowly over her until his body blocked the sun. Ellen felt the rough blanket on her back and Pete's warm lips on hers.

She found the hem of his shirt and pulled it off, only breaking the kiss for a moment. Then she grabbed the hem of her shirt and wriggled beneath Pete as she kissed him while getting free of all her clothes. It suddenly seemed as if they couldn't shed their clothes fast enough. Making love with Pete under the blue December sky made her feel exposed and vulnerable, but she wasn't turning back from the pure electricity racing over their heated skin.

With Pete kissing her neck and sending waves of desire over her body, Ellen tuned out any thoughts of caution. Not just her friend now, he was six feet of sexy man. How had she never allowed herself this delicious pleasure before?

It was reckless, but if Pete did leave the island and break her heart, she didn't want to wonder the rest of her life what she had missed.

****

As the sun began to set on her twenty-fifth birthday, Ellen helped fold their blanket and pick up the wrappers and cans from their snacks. Making love with her best friend, no matter what the future might bring, had been the best way to celebrate a quarter of a century so far.

And the next quarter of a century? Ellen pushed the thought from her mind and focused on the present. She noticed the pink and orange streaks of light in the western sky, colorful clouds hanging over the mainland. It would be a nice evening to fly or be on the water, but she was on her beloved island with the person she most wanted to be with.

"Dinnertime," Pete said. "I know you have to be hungry."

"I'm actually pretty satisfied," she said, giggling.

"For food, I mean."

She smiled. "I could eat several plates of almost anything."

"I'll drive."

Pete steered the golf cart off the beach and onto the narrow asphalt road surrounding the island. Instead of heading for downtown, Pete turned the opposite direction toward the more isolated end of the island.

"There's only one restaurant this way," Ellen commented.

"Since we're on a romantic date, I thought we'd go to the winery. I may even tell them it's your birthday so the waiters will sing to you, and they'll bring you one of those tiny cakes with a single candle in it."

"My parents offered me dinner and birthday cake if I wanted to eat in the formal dining room at the hotel with them, but I told them I was going out with you."

Pete glanced sideways at her. "What did they say?"

"Nothing. It didn't seem weird to them that I'd be with you."

Of course it wasn't weird. She and Pete had been like peanut butter and jelly their whole lives.

"I'm glad you chose me," Pete said.

"Me, too."

"I asked my parents to let Edison out and give him his supper. They weren't surprised since I always spend your birthday with you."

"Did you tell them what time you'd be home?"

Pete grinned. "Nope."

They pulled into the winery and parked with other cars and golf carts. Most tourists left their cars at home, but a few drove them onto the car ferry owned by a company in Oceanview that made a daily round trip. And many islanders had cars. Except for Ellen. With a hotel van, a ferry, and an airplane at her disposal, she'd never seen the need for one. Pete's family owned a pickup and a trailer, but they usually only used it for picking up golf carts when tourists got flat tires or dead batteries somewhere on the island.

Pete put his arm around her as they walked up the steps to the patio seating. Red and green candles decorated the tables. Although it was a Sunday evening, there were dozens of other diners because the holiday season was a busy time on the island. Ellen sat in her chair when Pete pulled it out for her. He took the chair across the small table from her.

"I heard they had some additions to their menu," Ellen said. "They got a new chef, someone new to the island. I overheard someone in our kitchen at the hotel talking about it."

"If the food is good, you can steal the chef for the Grand," Pete commented, a grin lighting his face and eyes.

"The kitchen is not my wheelhouse. And it's nice having some place other than the family hotel to have a good meal. Just in case I want to go on a date."

I'm on a date. And I just had fabulous birthday sex. She perused the wine menu that was already on the table. Perhaps wine would steady her nerves and quell the force running through her veins.

The waitress dropped off glasses of water and menus, promising to return shortly for their food and drink orders.

"I'm having seafood," Pete announced. "And I'm paying for dinner."

"Because we're on a date?" Ellen said, lowering her voice as she finished the question.

Pete leaned close across the table. "You don't have to whisper. Unless you're ashamed of being out with me."

She laughed. "Not at all. People are probably thinking you could do better for a date than the resident island tomboy."

"No, I couldn't. Besides, it's your birthday."

"I'll return the favor on yours," she said. And then her heart dipped inside her chest. Pete's birthday was the fifth of June, six months away. Even though it was the height of tourist season, she and Pete had always found time to celebrate it. She had given him aerial photographs of the island and his golf cart business last year, digital copies he could use for his website and a framed one to hang up. When she'd chosen that gift, she'd thought Pete was totally invested in the family business. There to stay.

Where would he be on his next birthday? And would they celebrate it together?

"I can guess your thoughts," Pete said. He was staring at her over the top of his menu.

"I was thinking about your birthday next summer. If your business sells and you're working on the mainland, what will you do on June fifth?"

"I think you're taking me out to dinner," he said. "You'll owe me after tonight."

Ellen sighed. Her eyes were on the menu with its gorgeous pictures and descriptions, but her thoughts robbed her appetite.

"What will you do…over there?"

Pete laughed. "You make it sound like I'm going to another country. Or another continent."

"Will you get your own place? Get a job in electricity?"

He scooted his chair back and crossed one leg over the other. "I don't know. I sent out some resumes and already got one bite. I may go interview this week if the timing works out. I could bunk with my sister until I find my own place."

"Tell me about the job you're interviewing for." She wasn't sure she wanted to hear about something that would take Pete away, but he was her best friend. She had to listen.

"It's with a small firm that's starting to make a name for itself. I think they liked my resume because I have an electrical engineering degree, but I also have experience running a business. Project management and budgeting is a big deal in small business. They're doing a lot of work in new construction in Oceanview since the hotel and restaurant scene is really expanding over there."

Ellen smiled, but didn't say anything.

"Am I talking too much?" Pete asked.

She shook her head. "Of course not. I want to hear your plans, and it sounds really exciting." *She had to ask.* "Is this what you want?"

"When I moved to this island when I was in kindergarten, I felt like the new kid until you sat next to me at lunch during the first week of school."

"I remember that," Ellen said. She could still picture him, the only boy at the island school the other kids had never seen before.

"I don't think my family ever planned to stay as long as we did. My dad took the job managing the former golf cart rental place because he needed a job. And this one came with housing and a decent place for his kids to grow up. He bought it a long time ago thinking he'd have something valuable to sell when my sister and I were grown up. And now we are."

"And you can be free," she said.

Pete reached across the table and put his hand over Ellen's. "I didn't ask for this," he said. "I didn't ask for my parents to move here twenty years ago, and I didn't ask them to pull the rug out from under my feet now."

"Why don't you tell them that?"

"Because they think they're doing what I've always wanted. You've heard it yourself, my yapping on and on about getting an electrical engineering job on the mainland as soon as I can get away from the island. You've always dreamed of staying right where you are, but I always dreamed of proving myself on my own."

"Different dreams," Ellen whispered. Her throat was thick. Of course she'd heard Pete talk about leaving the island, but she had never believed he would—until now. And now she had the most to lose.

Chapter Six

The next afternoon, Ellen waited by the gangplank of the Grand Hotel's yacht *The Faire Catherine*. Named after her grandmother, the meticulously restored 1950 Chris Craft wooden boat was all Hollywood elegance. Guests could commission a two-hour tour around the island aboard the forty-foot vessel, weather permitting, and it was one of Ellen's favorite jobs. She had taken out engaged couples, newlyweds, anniversary couples, and families. Sometimes a professional photographer came along to take pictures of the guests, especially with the island or the historic lighthouse in the background.

The boat was fueled up. Running. Stocked with food and drinks.

But no one was showing up.

She checked for messages on her cell phone. A new one from her cousin Cora at the front desk confirmed what Ellen already suspected. Her afternoon tour had canceled at the last minute. The hotel guests would lose their deposit money, which had already been used to fuel the boat. And it seemed like a shame to return the boat to its slip in the marina without enjoying the sunny December day.

Pete, his white t-shirt catching the sun, waved to her from up the hill. He stood in front of a short row of golf carts, probably the only ones still available on a high-volume tourist day. She waved back, wishing she had time to spend with him during the busy holiday season. Especially if this was their last.

She brushed that sad thought from her mind and replaced it with a wonderful idea. *He did not look busy.* She swiped his number on her cell phone.

"Pete's famous fortune-telling service. I'm sensing you are very lonely. Or you need a golf cart."

"I need a playmate," Ellen said.

"I'm in."

"You don't even know what I'm asking you to do."

"That's the fun part. The thrill of the unknown," Pete said.

"My afternoon island tour canceled at the last minute. My boat is running and loaded with food, snacks, and champagne."

"See how right I was?"

Ellen laughed. "Can you sneak away for two hours?"

"Putting a closed sign in the window as we speak."

"Don't do that," Ellen said. "What will your parents say?"

"Kidding. My dad's hanging out in the office anyway. I'll just ask him to manage without me while I bail a friend out of a terrible situation."

"You're a great guy."

"I know. It's a burden. One question, though. Can I bring Edison? He loves a boat ride."

"Of course. Come as soon as you can. I'll be waiting."

"You have no idea how sexy that sounded," Pete said.

Ellen entered the cool cabin of the boat. The elegant wood interior was softened with dark green cushions—all of them embroidered with the trademark of the hotel, a pine tree with a gold GH. It was formal and elegant, but it was still a boat. Made for fun. Especially with the stock of fruit, chocolates, nuts, pastries, and champagne she found in the fridge.

That fruit won't keep, she reasoned. And the champagne wouldn't last if opened.

She had every intention of opening it.

As soon as Pete stepped foot on her boat, she felt the vessel dip gently toward the dock. She turned in time to see him enter the cabin and cross it in two long strides. He pulled her into his arms and rocked the boat with his quick movements. His yellow Labrador followed him and greeted Ellen by licking her knee.

"It's been forever since last night," Pete said. "Longest day of my life."

"I agree," she said. "I feel like I'm a year older than I was two days ago." She kissed him, letting her lips and tongue explore.

Pete glanced around the cabin. "I've never been aboard this boat, but even a first timer can see that those cushions look inviting," he said. "I could ask Edison to step out on the back deck so we can have privacy. He can be bought off with a bowl of water and two or more dog treats."

Ellen laughed. "We're in the marina with too many prying eyes. If the boat starts rocking too much, our secret will be out."

"Then let's go someplace where no one will notice," Pete said. "Not that I care what people think."

"Of course you don't," Ellen said. "You're leaving. I have to live here."

Her tone said she was joking, but her words betrayed her true thoughts. Pete drew his eyebrows together and ran a hand over her hair.

"I'm sorry," he said.

She shook her head. "Don't be. Let's not think about it today. We have a two hour boat ride ahead of us, and I expect you to help me eat those chocolate covered strawberries."

He still had a serious expression, regret taking away the joy in his eyes.

"Captain's orders," Ellen said. "Don't make me toss you overboard."

His smile returned. "I wouldn't dream of it. I'll go throw off the shore lines and then we'll work together on the champagne and dessert problem you seem to have."

****

Pete had always felt as if he lived right on the edge of a fairy tale. A peripheral character, witness to the interesting and elegant lives of others. But not the kind of hero who got the girl. Standing next to Ellen at the wheel of the spectacular boat her family owned, he felt as if he had moved a few pages closer to a storybook ending.

"Any chance you'll let me drive?" he asked. He didn't expect her to say yes. The *Faire Catherine* was probably priceless, every detail historically accurate right down to the hum of the motors below the deck. He expected to see movie stars in white linen pants strolling the deck.

"Sure," she said, moving aside and gesturing toward the wheel. "I let kids drive when I take out families. It's easy to steer when we're out in open water. And parents love taking pictures of their children playing captain."

"I feel really special right now."

Ellen laughed. "I could take your picture and text it to your mom if it would make you feel better."

"Paybacks are hell," he commented as he took the wheel and focused on the horizon. "My mom would probably invite you over for meatloaf. Especially if I told her how much you love it."

"I never suspected you of having a mean streak."

"It's the salty air."

Ellen stood behind him and put her arms around his waist.

"Don't tell me you do that with all your passengers, too."

He felt the rumble of her laughter. "Depends how well they tip."

It was very difficult to concentrate on the elaborate ship's wheel with Ellen's arms around him. Pete cleared his throat. "Will you be my date to the island Christmas party tomorrow night?"

"Of course," she said. *No hesitation. Definitely a good sign.* "I plan to tell everyone you were my birthday present this year."

He laughed. "Makes those sunglasses seem like overkill." He'd noticed she was wearing them when he got on the boat, but they were now on the driver's console.

"Not at all. I got two fantastic presents."

They had already passed the downtown harbor and shopping area and the island shoreline was now dominated by the pine trees that had given it its name. As Pete steered around the quiet northern shore of the island, it felt as if they were almost alone on an ocean.

"We've come a long way since our first attempt at boating together when we were thirteen," Pete said.

Ellen moved next to him and he saw her broad smile. "The July Fourth Boat Parade. We failed the first year, but we redeemed ourselves a lot the next three."

Pete vividly remembered raiding what Ellen called the Grand Hotel junk yard. With a bathtub from a former remodel and a patio umbrella that was faded and thrown out, they thought they had a seaworthy vessel. No matter how pathetic it looked and how dire their parents' warnings were.

"We would have been all right if Tesla hadn't decided to swim out from shore and jump in," Ellen said. "That's what tipped the tub and sank it."

"He was a good dog," Pete said. "But he tended to overestimate his swimming ability. I wonder if divers will someday find our bathtub on the bottom of the Atlantic."

Ellen giggled. "They'll wonder what happened."

"We should try it again sometime, especially since my current dog is a much better swimmer."

Despite their first failure, Pete and Ellen had built and entered an increasingly sophisticated homemade boat the next several years. It was only one in a long string of happy memories with his best friend on White Pine Island.

But if Pete did leave the island, it was also one of the many things he would almost certainly never do again.

"Lighthouse coming up around this next bend," Ellen said. "We usually have to pause there for pictures when I take people out."

Pete slid an arm around her. "We could stop for a while. I have a pocket full of treats for Edison."

When the dog heard his name, he picked up his head and gave Pete a look of loyalty and affection. Edison licked Pete's ankle and put his head down again, closing his eyes and apparently enjoying the feel of the boat's motor humming underneath him.

"We do have an anchor," Ellen said. "And I know where there's a little cove with plenty of bottom clearance and no boat traffic."

Ellen took the wheel and steered the boat into a cove while Pete made sure his dog was happy and shaded on the deck outside the cabin. He came in the back door of the elegant wooden cabin at the same time Ellen came in the front door near where she had been steering the boat. They stood, facing each other. Pete felt his heartbeat in his throat.

"You know," Ellen said. "I've never had sex on this boat."

"I don't believe that," Pete said, laughing. "This is the sexiest boat I've ever seen."

"I'm not saying it hasn't been done," she said. "Just not by me. Yet."

They met in the middle of the cabin, each of them already pulling off clothing. In the quiet secluded cove, there was no one to notice the rhythmic rocking of the boat.

Chapter Seven

Ellen's phone jolted her out of bed at four o'clock in the morning. Pete had taken her home the night before, stayed long enough to remind her why she didn't ever want him to leave, and gone home around midnight. How was she ever going to let him go now that he'd been in her bed and made her feel things she'd never felt before?

She was making a mess of everything.

"Hello?" she said.

"Sorry, Ellen." It was her Uncle Charles who co-owned the Grand Hotel. "I've got a guest with an emergency who needs to get to the mainland right now."

Ellen was already out of bed, bedroom light on, searching for clothing.

"Medical emergency?"

She'd flown those before. The small island medical center had called in her help numerous times when medical care was necessary but not serious enough to call the medical helicopter from the Oceanview Hospital.

"Not the guest. But her sister was in an accident outside Oceanview and is in bad shape."

"Ready in five minutes," Ellen said.

"The van is on its way to get you so you can warm up the plane. I'll drive the guest up myself in the next half hour."

She put down the phone, brushed her teeth, tossed on appropriate clothing, and flipped on her porch lights. Both lights worked, thanks to Pete, making it easier for the hotel van to navigate the dark driveway in front of her cottage.

Yauncey smiled at her as she hopped in the passenger seat. She wasn't surprised to see him. He and his wife lived in a small bungalow behind the hotel and were always on hand. They'd worked there nearly forty years.

"Don't you ever get any sleep?" she asked.

"I'll sleep when I'm dead," he said. "Seatbelt. I don't see very well in the dark."

Great. I hope they have the lights on at the airport.

The airport was dark when they arrived. Ellen turned on the runway lights and rolled her plane out of its hangar. She performed a pre-flight check, radioed the tower on the mainland with her flight plan, and waited. Her Uncle Charlie drove onto the narrow runway, straight to her plane, and shook hands with the departing guests, sending them on their way with condolences and well wishes.

Two hours later, as Ellen returned to the island and landed on the small strip, she thought about how many times she'd made emergency runs in her plane. She hadn't saved lives, at least not by herself, but she made a difference in the lives of the people who called White Pine Island home. It was her home, too. The evening before, she had considered, for a brief moment, what it would be like to follow Pete to the mainland and start a new life. A life outside of her family business.

That seemed to be what he wanted, to be his own man.

But that was never what she wanted for herself. The Grand Hotel was in her blood. The people there were her blood. She was important to them. They mattered to her.

There was no way she could leave…even if it meant giving up Pete.

Did she have to give up Pete, just because he would live on the mainland and work there? The reality of the situation kept her awake as she tried to take a quick nap before moving on to her shift running the morning ferry. She couldn't sleep, so she tried to study the manual for her commercial pilot's license. She had the hours and experience, and now all she had to do was take a test. A very hard test.

She had too much on her mind right now with Pete. And the holidays. And Pete.

After taking the morning ferry runs, she returned to the hotel and helped her parents ready the ball room for the island Christmas party. The giant tree and several smaller ones were already up. Ellen's parents knew she didn't have a decorating gift, so they put her in charge of the slightly more industrial jobs. Moving tables. Setting up chairs. Digging decorations out of storage. Helping her cousin Samantha when something needed to be done on a ladder.

It would be a great party. And she would have a date for the first time in her life. But what about next year?

"What are you wearing?" Samantha asked as she untangled a string of colored lights.

Ellen shrugged. "I never put away the dress I wore to the wedding a few nights ago."

Samantha screwed up her face and cocked her head at her cousin. "If I had your gorgeous blond hair instead of my red hair, I would absolutely wear red for a Christmas party."

"I don't have a red dress."

"I do. I bought it on an epic shopping trip with my mother last year. In the fluorescent lights at the department store, we both thought it looked great with my hair. In the real light of day...not so much."

"I can't take your dress," Ellen said. If she knew her cousin and her aunt, the dress was probably much more fashionable and fancy than anything in her own little closet.

"It still has the tags on it," Samantha said. "But I lost the receipt and I hate returning stuff anyway. I'm serious. I'm not using it, we wear the same size, and I know you have black heels that will look great."

Ellen grinned at her cousin. "Can I come over and try it on?"

"Just as soon as you attach the end of this string of lights to that hook on the ceiling. I'd rather show up naked at the party than climb a ladder. And while you're trying your party dress on, I expect a full report on what's happening between you and Pete."

"You know about that?"

Samantha smiled. "I do now. I had only suspected until you just confirmed it."

Ellen went home, showered, spent quality time on her hair and makeup, and slithered into the borrowed red dress. She took a hard look at herself in the long mirror tacked to the back of her bedroom door. Even with the high black heels, she'd still be six inches shorter than Pete. She pictured herself with her head on his shoulder as they danced. She put on a pair of flats and walked down the hill to the Grand Hotel, her party shoes dangling from her hand. It was already dark, and the hotel lights were a festive beacon. She followed the sounds of the orchestra as the usual thrill went through her when she walked into her family's elegant hotel.

Her life on the island was a fairy tale, and she never wanted reality to wake her up. But the hero of her personal story was leaving, and she had an impossible decision to make. She tucked her flats behind the front desk and slid into her heels. She'd think about that decision *after* the holiday party.

The first person Ellen saw as she entered the ballroom was her younger brother Easton who had just come in on the afternoon ferry. Home for the holidays from college, he was already dancing with a girl, drink in hand. Her parents took the twenty-one rule very seriously, probably because they didn't want to lose their liquor license, and this was the first holiday party hosted at the Grand where her brother was allowed a libation.

Easton, tall like his older brother Ned, waved at Ellen with his drink hand. Amazingly, it didn't appear to Ellen that he spilled a drop. Each of the Phillips kids possessed a talent. Ned golfed, Ellen loved being behind the wheel, and Kate was warm and nurturing. But Easton was music in motion. He'd played with the Grand Hotel orchestra since he was twelve, and his future as a musician or conductor seemed like a certainty. He was majoring in music, but Ellen fully expected him to spend his career in the Grand Hotel orchestra, playing daily for guests, coordinating entertainment, and wowing the islanders with an occasional concert.

Ellen's parents cultivated their children's talents, but Ellen also knew they hoped Ellen's generation would want to stay on the island and use those talents in the family business. Her cousins Samantha, Grant, Mike, and Cora each had a gift in the hospitality niche. Together, the Phillips family was ready to keep the Grand Hotel's elegant lights on for at least another generation.

"You're here," Pete said. She felt his breath on her bare shoulders as he spoke. The dress exposed her shoulders, arms, and plenty of leg. She was torn between hoping Pete would find her irresistible—and fearing he would. "When you suggested we meet here instead of letting me pick you up, I was almost afraid you'd ditch me and change the oil in your airplane or something."

Ellen turned. They were so close they could kiss. Could they kiss in front of everyone? So far, only Samantha knew that things had changed between Ellen and Pete. Dramatically. Ellen had told her cousin everything, especially her fear of what would happen next. Ever the optimist about other people's love lives, Samantha had shrugged and said they'd find a way if it was meant to be.

Would they find a way?

"We're not going to shake hands or fist bump are we?" Pete asked.

Ellen put her palms on both his cheeks and kissed him quickly on the lips. She felt as if she'd just taken the first bubbly sip of champagne but there was an entire bottle left just for her.

"Better than a hand shake," Pete said. His Adam's apple bobbed up and down and his cheeks were flushed.

"I like your suit," Ellen said. She held Pete at arm's length so she could see all of him. The last time she'd seen him in a suit was probably last year's Christmas party. But a lot had changed since then. Last year, he was her co-

conspirator forced to dress up for a holiday party but looking forward to taking his dress shoes off at the end of the night. They'd watched television and snacked on party leftovers on her couch.

This year, he was her date. And they were looking forward to going back to her place at the end of the night for an entirely different reason.

"You are beautiful," Pete said. His eyes lingered on the red dress with just enough plunge to the neckline to make it interesting.

"I borrowed the dress from my cousin Sam," Ellen said.

"I'll have to thank her when I see her."

Ellen swallowed. Pete's predatory gaze was making waves of heat shimmer and pool all over her body.

"Let's sample the food," Ellen suggested, taking his hand and leading him toward the long tables filled with elegant finger foods and desserts. She handed him a small white plate with gold letters spelling out the hotel's name. They filled their plates as they moved down the table. Mini-cheesecakes. Water chestnuts. Shrimp. Fancy cheese. Ornately decorated cookies. Truffles.

As they picked up dinner napkins and searched for a high-top table to set their plates on, they found a table for four with only two places taken.

Ned and Bethany stood at the tall table with plates of food in front of them, but their eyes were on each other. Ned wore a black suit, and Bethany wore a stunning royal blue cocktail dress.

"Should we?" Pete whispered to Ellen.

"No, but let's do it anyway," she whispered back.

When Ellen and Pete's plates clinked softly onto the cloth-covered table, Ned and Bethany startled like wild animals and glanced up.

"Sorry to interrupt," Ellen said.

"No, you're not," Ned said.

"Not interrupting?"

Ned glowered at his younger sister. "Not sorry."

Ellen shrugged and gave Bethany a quick hug. "Your dress is beautiful," she said.

Bethany smiled. "Better than the pink bridesmaid dress?"

Ellen bit her lip, not sure if she should laugh and commiserate or keep a professional expression appropriate for her role as the owning family of the hotel. While she hesitated, Ned and Pete shook hands and started eating. Although Ned was two years older than Ellen and Pete, they'd run in the same circle of island kids all their lives. Been to the same school, the same weddings and funerals, the same parties. Shared a beer at Chuck's with the other locals, and attended this dress-up party every year.

"I think this dress is better for a holiday party," Ellen said.

Bethany laughed aloud. "I felt like a cupcake in that pink dress, but my sister insisted." She popped a truffle into her mouth.

"I hope she was happy with her wedding experience here," Ellen said.

"Thrilled. Which is definitely saying something as she is notoriously tough to please."

From what Ellen had heard and seen from Priscilla, that was an understatement.

"We should dance," Ellen suggested.

Pete groaned. "We're in for it," he said to Bethany. "Kids who grow up in a Grand Hotel know all the ballroom moves. Swing. Rumba. All that stuff."

"I've tried to teach you," Ellen said to Pete.

"I was never sufficiently motivated," he said. "But maybe tonight's the night."

Ned raised both eyebrows and smirked at his sister. She grabbed Pete's hand and led him to the dance floor, hoping the orchestra would keep playing the swing music mixed with some peppy Christmas tunes. She could lead Pete through a few steps, repeat them, and keep her emotions under control.

No luck.

As soon as she stepped onto the wood dance floor with Pete, the Grand Hotel orchestra began a medley of slow holiday songs. *Blue Christmas. What are you doing New Year's Eve?* And worst of all, *I'll be home for Christmas.*

Maudlin holiday songs that could only be slow-shuffled to on the dance floor. Ellen placed a hand on Pete's shoulder, but he pulled her close anyway. She glanced around the dance floor. Other couples were eating up the holiday dirge. The older couple who owned the grocery store downtown were glued together, her white head on his shoulder. The son of the family that managed the winery was locked in with a girl who worked the front desk at another hotel on the island.

There was no choice. Ellen and Pete's hands were clasped, her left in his right. They began to move together. His body brushed hers all the way down the front. His cheek touched hers. Holiday lights swirled around them. She was dancing with her new lover in a room with nearly every single person on earth she knew. She caught a glimpse of some of their faces as she turned in slow circles, moving around the dance floor to the orchestra's music.

There was her mother talking with her aunt. Pete's parents chatting with Yauncey. The airport manager. The dock master. A long-time housekeeper at the hotel. Chuck and his wife, mainland Marian, who looked like a flight risk as her eyes darted around the venue.

Everyone was there. And a realization hit Ellen. Everyone knew. Her feelings for Pete had to be written on her face. She snuck a look at him. Written on his face, too. There was no hiding it.

She didn't want to hide it. She was in love with Pete McCormack. Not just the casual "love you" as they disconnected a phone call. The real deal. No matter what.

She had to tell him. She swallowed. Straightened her spine. Looked him in the eye.

"Pete, I—"

"Can I cut in?"

Her mouth hung open with the unspoken words. Pete's expression turned to shock.

She knew that voice behind her. With one last look at Pete, she turned around and faced Alex, the one other man she'd given her heart to.

He held his arms wide. "I'm back for the holidays," he announced in a voice that suggested he was sure of his welcome. "Visiting the family, having a few laughs for old times' sake." He clearly expected Ellen to step into his arms for a reunion hug.

But she couldn't. This was the man who'd left the island, stopped calling, and maintained total silence for over three years. Ellen glanced over his shoulder and saw her mother's face. Rebecca Phillips was always nice to everyone, especially when a difficult situation demanded careful words. She was the undisputed queen of social grace. However, her expression right now could be translated as "kick him in the junk, Ellen, and walk away with your head high."

Ellen locked eyes with her mother long enough to say thank you for the unspoken advice. Instead of using her pointy-toed shoes, though, she crossed her arms over her chest. She felt Pete move in closer behind her, his heat radiating along her back.

"You can't be mad at me," Alex said. "So I left your precious island. I had a right to my own life, didn't I?"

Maybe her mother was right.

"And anyway, I'm back for Christmas. I thought we could get the old gang together, have some fun."

Ellen was speechless. The last thing she wanted to do was hang out with Alex. He'd humiliated her. Made her take a chance on turning friendship into a physical relationship. Made her some promises about continuing that relationship even though he was leaving White Pine Island. And made her miserable for months as she waited for the calls that eventually stopped coming.

Pete reached around her and shook hands with Alex. "I hope you have a nice holiday with your family," he said.

How can he be so nice? The irony of the situation hit Ellen like a sleigh full of toys. Pete and Alex had something in common. They had a lot of things in common.

But one thing they weren't going to share was the ability to leave her and break her heart.

"Pete's leaving the island, too," she said suddenly. "Maybe you can give him some tips on surviving in the real world."

Ellen shoved off from Pete, marched straight past Alex, and headed for the exit. Her cousin Samantha threaded arms with her as she left the dance floor. "I was just going outside for some fresh air," Samantha said, as she fell into step beside Ellen.

Chapter Eight

Like a man fighting a strong current, knowing he'll never make it to shore, Pete slogged his way through the party guests and followed Ellen and Samantha. His feet were leaden, but he was determined. He had to find Ellen and erase the damage their former friend had done. Erase the cold lines that had settled on her face.

He heard them talking, heard the porch rockers creaking. And heard just one word from Ellen that summed up the past few crazy wonderful days. *Mistake.* She said it loud and clear. Pete stopped in front of the two women and leaned on the porch rail.

"I'm not a mistake, Ellen. I'm more than that."

"Of course you are," she said, her voice uneven. "I love you, Pete. I was just about to tell you that when Alex interrupted us."

Pete slid to his knees in front of Ellen's chair and took both her hands.

"But that's exactly why I have to let you go," she said.

His breath caught. She loved him. But what was she saying?

"What do you mean when you say you're letting me go?"

Ellen withdrew her hands and sat back in the chair. Pete felt marooned, kneeling on the hard wooden planks of the porch floor. Worse than feeling adrift, he felt foolish. As if he'd made a drastic and irrevocable mistake.

"When you leave and start a new life in Oceanview or wherever you end up, I don't want you to feel like you left a trail of mud behind you."

Like Alex.

"Are we talking about me or Alex here, because we're not the same."

"I know you're not the same. I don't want you to feel unwelcome if you ever do come back. That's why I'm letting the past few days go. Pretending they didn't happen."

"But they happened. And I can't forget," Pete said. There was no way he could go back to friend status, not after what he'd experienced with Ellen. Having someone who knew you inside and out and loved you, and then having that love turn to passion and deeper love? There was no way he was going to sail away from White Pine Island with a clean slate. He didn't want to.

"It's better this way," Ellen said. "We've been friends for twenty years and lovers for three days. Certainly we can…rewind."

Her voice was still small, sounding far away as if he was talking with her over a phone with an unstable connection.

"Rewind?" Pete said incredulously. He rose to his feet and backed away from Ellen, shock making his legs heavy.

"I'm going to get out of the way here," Samantha said. She stood and her chair rocked with the movement.

"Stay," Ellen said. "We're all friends here. We can complain about what a jerk Alex is, the way he waltzed in here after four years and thought we were going to fall all over him. Like we've always done."

That's what they would have done, Pete thought. Until he became Ellen's lover, he'd have sat next to her, refilled her glass, and joined in the crab session about their insensitive former friend.

But the situation had changed. And Pete was afraid that every word out of his mouth might be used against him in the future, if he went down the same path Alex did.

"You can't just dismiss me," Pete said. "Dismiss *us* as if nothing has changed. I love you, Ellen. I always have."

"If you love me, you'll go back to being my best friend before you leave the island. That will make it easier. For both of us."

"I can't do that. And neither can you," Pete said. Exasperated, he turned and stalked the length of the long elegant porch, leaving the island Christmas party angry and unsatisfied for the first time in his life. He slid into his golf cart and drove down the hill without turning the headlights on. He knew the way, even in the dark, but it was the only thing in his life he was sure of.

****

The next morning, Pete was up early checking batteries and wiping spider webs off his lineup of golf carts. He'd given up sleeping and watched the dawn come slowly to the island. It was exactly one week until Christmas, and the uptick in tourist traffic was typical. Holiday travelers took daytrips to White Pine Island as part of their family vacation. Some came to the island to stay. Just yesterday, he'd greeted two groups who'd come nearly every year and rented a golf cart from his family's business. He knew them by name.

He was going to miss that. Miss the familiarity, the island, the sunshine glancing off the water. Did he really want to trade in island life? But what choice did he have? Pete saw his father walking out of the office and heading his way. He planned to tell his dad he had a job interview very early the next morning and would be taking the last ferry and spending the night on the mainland with his sister.

But his dad was flushed with excitement, his step quick as he approached.

"Got a call from a man who wants to come see our business later today. Checking it out, sounds like a potentially serious buyer," Pete's dad said. Pete finished wiping down the windshield of a cart while he listened. "Can't believe someone saw our ad already and is coming tonight." The older man hadn't looked this happy or hopeful since the day he was declared cancer free months ago.

"Your mother and I are just so glad we're finally letting you out of obligations so you can do what you want, son. It's all we ever wanted for you and your sister. And you've had it harder, having to run things for us."

"You know I don't see it as an obligation, dad. But I'm glad to hear there's interest from a buyer. What time is the man coming?"

"Late. He's coming over on the six o'clock ferry. May end up staying the night on the island. We're counting on you to tell him all the details of the business and show him what a good investment it would be for him. Your mother is going to cook something special since he's probably going to be here for dinner. She's thinking meatloaf."

Pete smiled. He hoped to miss dinner, but of course he'd be there to help his parents sell the family business. However, it meant he'd have to find a way to the mainland very early the next morning long before the ferries began their daily schedule. And there was only one person he could think of to ask.

"Say," his dad said. "Would you call Ellen and see if they could save a room at the Grand, just in case? With all the tourists, I don't want to take a chance."

Pete nodded. "I was going to call her anyway tonight."

"She's a sweetheart," his dad said, and then he walked away whistling a holiday tune.

****

Ellen spent the day after the Christmas party dodging everyone she knew. The only person who knew the whole story was Samantha, but there was no point in rehashing everything with her again. They'd been over it last night after Pete stomped off the porch. Ned hadn't said a word, and Ellen hoped he was too busy with Bethany to notice what happened at the party. He'd certainly remember Alex and the effect of his departure several years back, but Ellen wondered if he would put together the connection between that incident and what was happening now between her and Pete.

Her mother was the most difficult bullet to outrun. Ellen knew her mother noticed the fact that she was there with Pete as a date. And she saw the return of the prodigal Alex. And the subsequent hurried exit Ellen made. No doubt her mother had done the math and would provide an ear or a shoulder to cry on.

But Ellen's feelings were too close to the surface. If she started pouring out her heart to her mother, she'd end up in the well-stocked wine cellar with a box of tissues. Instead, she planned to keep her head down and her heart distracted. It was the holiday season with plenty of action. Certainly she could manage to forget she'd accidentally fallen in love with her best friend just as she was about to lose him forever.

After docking the six o'clock ferry, Ellen descended to the passenger area to help passengers disembark with their groups and their luggage. Most people coming to the island that late in the day had plans to stay overnight, and Ellen made a point of helping guests of the Grand Hotel as well as those of the other hotels and bed and breakfasts on the island. What was good for one hotel was good for all of them.

A middle-aged man, apparently traveling alone, pulled a small overnight bag on wheels.

"Can I help you find where you're going?" Ellen asked. She assumed he was joining his family at a hotel or staying with friends on the island.

The man turned to Ellen and smiled. He was attractive with a wide white smile. She had never seen him before.

"I'm looking for McCormack Golf Cart Rentals," he said.

Ellen pointed up the hill. "It's the only cart rental on the island," she said. "Easy to find."

"The only one? That does sweeten the deal."

"What deal?" she asked, curiosity overtaking manners.

"It's for sale," he explained. "And if it has no competitors, it's more likely to be a good investment."

"Oh."

"At least that's what I'm here to find out. Thanks for your help." He walked away with his rolling bag bumping along behind him.

Ellen's phone rang and she saw Pete's picture on the screen. She could do this. She could pretend they were friends. They *were* friends.

"Seasick boat captains anonymous," she said.

"Boat captains can't get seasick," he said.

"That's why they have to stay anonymous. It's embarrassing."

"Poor devils. Els, I know I have no right to ask you anything, especially not today, but I may need a favor."

"What do you mean especially not today?"

There was a long pause on Pete's end of the call. "Because of what happened last night."

Ellen swallowed. If she could pretend nothing had happened, she should probably ask her parents to build a theater in the hotel so she could tread the boards.

"Rewind," she said. "A few days. Pretend it's last Friday and ask me your favor. I'm busy running the ferry right now."

"I can see you from my office. You're standing on the dock. By yourself."

"Stalker," Ellen said. "Now what do you want? I already know you have a buyer looking at your business and probably staying the night. Does he need a hotel room?"

"Possibly, if you have one you could save. And thank you. But I also need a ride to the mainland at seven tomorrow morning."

"Ferry starts at ten."

"I was hoping you could fly me over to Oceanview," he said. Ellen could hear him breathing on the other end of the line. "I have a job interview early in the morning."

Ellen picked up a dock rope and twirled it. *So much for hiding from my problems.*

"I see you twirling that rope," Pete said. "I hope you're not thinking of tying me up and throwing me overboard."

"So," she said, "you need a hotel room for the guy who may buy your business and a ride for yourself to get a job off this island."

"Perfect storm," Pete said. "I'm sorry. If you don't want to do it, I'll borrow a kayak and start rowing tonight. You have every right to tell me to go to hell."

How could she help him leave when it was the last thing she wanted? But how could she refuse to help him when she loved him so much it hurt?

"No, I don't. You're my oldest friend, and you're only doing what you said you would. Be at the airport at seven, and give the buyer a ride to the Grand tonight if he misses the last ferry."

****

Although it was only four miles from the tiny airstrip at the highest elevation of White Pine Island to the somewhat larger airport outside Oceanview, Pete thought it might be the longest flight of his life. Ellen had greeted him cheerfully. Stowed his briefcase safely behind the seat. Snapped on her seatbelt and taxied down the runway with complete professionalism. Cold professionalism. As if she were flying a complete stranger to the store to pick out wallpaper for his spare bathroom.

They'd already discussed the weather. Fair skies, seasonable temperatures. Perfect for holiday travelers who were on their way to the coastal region of Georgia to celebrate time off from work and school.

They'd discussed the potential buyer for the golf cart business who had demonstrated serious interest, stayed the night at the Grand Hotel, and would depart on a ferry sometime that day. Pete had no idea when they would hear back from him, but his parents were giddy and optimistic about their plans for the coming year.

They'd remarked on the new construction on the island—a housing development, a family-friendly resort, and a maintenance garage for the island-owned lawnmowers and trucks.

Pete thought he'd go crazy if they avoided the elephant sitting on the back seat of the airplane any longer.

"Are you nervous?" Ellen asked. "You're doing that thing where you torture your scalp with your fingers and then scrub your forehead with your fist."

Did she have to know him so well?

"Yes, I'm nervous. For some reason, all three partners want to meet with me. That's why it's this early. I feel like it'll be more a jury trial than a job interview."

"You'll be fine," Ellen said in the same way a mother might tell her kid to get on the school bus and quit his crying.

They were over the ocean now, flying low enough to see some early morning sailboats and fishing boats below. The mainland with sun reflecting off windows was right in front of them. Pete's stomach sank. Why was he doing this? Did he really want to leave the island? He'd visited Oceanview and traveled, of course, but only one place felt like home.

Only one person felt like home.

"I'd give it up for you," he said, turning to Ellen.

Ellen looked straight ahead, not acknowledging him. She began a slow circle around the Oceanview airport. Radioed the control tower. Made an elegant and controlled landing.

"Did you hear what I said?" Pete asked.

"There's a taxi waiting over there," she said, pointing.

"I mean it," he said. "You're more important to me than a job."

"It's not just a job," she said. "It's everything. Your family is leaving White Pine. Selling off the business, leaving you high and dry. You can't just decide to stay on an island where there's nothing for you."

He took her hand. "There's something for me."

She pulled her hand back. "Stop it, Pete. You know what I think? I think you're afraid you're going to blow it and not get the job, so you're using me as an excuse to not even try."

"That's not true." He knew she was only trying to protect herself by not listening to him. By not looking at him. But it hurt. Especially when he was willing to put everything on the line.

"I won't be the reason you screw up your life," she said. "I won't be the excuse for your fear of trying what you always said you wanted to do."

Pete felt as if he had been punched. "Is that what you really think?"

"Your taxi is waiting," she said, checking her wristwatch.

Pete got out of the plane, slammed the door, and stalked over to the taxi.

Chapter Nine

"Why are you on my ferry, Ned?" Ellen asked. Her tall handsome brother stood in the doorway of her wheelhouse two days before Christmas. Ellen had the first run of the day, leaving the island at ten and departing the mainland at eleven. Then leaving the island at noon and departing Oceanview at one. Back and forth, six round trips a day.

She should have been bored with it. Her life had so much sameness in it. But that's what she loved, the daily rhythm of island life matching the waves on the shore.

Ned grinned. "I'm in charge of taking Grandma Christmas shopping. Mom said it was because I'm the favorite grandchild."

"I'm sure that's it," Ellen said. "You can have the crown. I took her last year and we almost missed the last ferry of the day."

"Seriously?"

"Prepare to look at every single thing in every single store. Twice. And then be a beast of burden when she finally decides what her haul is going to be."

Ned leaned against the doorframe and put his chin on his chest.

"You should go sit with Grandma and go over her shopping list on the way to Oceanview. Might save you time later."

"She's downstairs talking with Mainland Marian. I think they're comparing lists."

"We're leaving the dock in five minutes and all passengers have to be below. Captain's orders," Ellen said.

Ned crossed his arms

"So how did Pete's job interview go?"

Ellen shrugged. "You're asking the wrong person."

"You haven't talked to him in three days?"

"I flew him over for his interview. And we didn't exactly part on good terms."

"Have you heard the news about the golf cart business?"

She nodded. "There's an offer on the table, but nobody knows details. At least nobody I've talked to. All hush-hush who the buyer is. I bet it's that guy who came and looked."

Ellen sounded the ferry's horn and signaled to the dockhands to throw off the lines. Ned was silent as she left the dock and the harbor. When she got out into open water, he stood next to her at the wheel, watching out the front window.

"You could make it work, you know," he said. "You and Pete."

"I don't want to talk about this."

"You love him. He loves you. What's the problem?"

Ellen flicked him a glance and returned to watching the water. "The problem is obvious. Relationships between people who don't live in the same place have disaster written all over them."

"If this is about Alex—"

"It's not."

"Good. Because I'd have to call you a moron if it were, and mom made me stop doing that when we were in junior high."

"Although Alex is an example of what I'm talking about. You can't have one person living on the island and one on the mainland."

"One of you could commute," Ned offered.

Ellen flicked him another glance.

"Not you, of course," he said.

"There's no way this will work out."

"If there was a way, would you want it to?"

"Of course I would, moron."

"I'm being serious," Ned said.

Ellen sighed. "Me, too. I finally realized I was in love with my best friend and, boom, he's leaving. My timing sucks."

Ned raised his eyebrows and shrugged. "Christmas miracle, maybe?"

"It would take a big one. Now go downstairs and make sure Grandma has something nice for me on her shopping list. I'd like flannel pajamas. Purple. Maybe matching slippers. Size seven."

If she was going to be lonely in her little house, she might as well be comfortable.

Throughout the day, as Ellen criss-crossed the Atlantic ferrying passengers back and forth between White Pine Island and Oceanview, she had plenty of time to think. She'd offered to take all the ferry runs that day so Jimmy could spend the day on the mainland with his wife's extended family in an early Christmas celebration. It was a decent tradeoff, she thought, and it would give her Christmas Eve all to herself.

Not that she wanted to be by herself. She knew exactly who she wanted by her side at the happiest time of the year, but she didn't know how she was going to get him there. With each nautical mile, her eyes opened wider. She began to realize a change in geography could not change her heart toward Pete. Especially since she had an airplane and a ferry at her fingertips.

Why hadn't she seen it before? The potential compromise allowing him a career on the mainland while she kept all the things she liked about her life.

Except her lonely bed. That could go.

Could it work? Was her brother right?

Ellen sighed as she pulled into the dock to pick up the nine o'clock and final run from Oceanview. If Pete were standing in front of her right now, she would wrap her tired arms around him and promise him she would do whatever it takes to keep him in her life.

She would tell him the only thing keeping her back was fear. And she'd slowly jettisoned her fear overboard with every wave she'd passed throughout the day.

Ellen docked the ferry and flipped on the deck lights so passengers wouldn't stumble as they entered or exited the boat. Because of the holiday season, several bright strands of Christmas lights decorated the ferry and the dock. The colored lights reflected off the oncoming passengers and their shopping bags. She watched the passengers boarding and grinned. Her brother Ned was barely recognizable under a heavy burden of boxes and bags, but she recognized her grandmother's quick step.

They really did shop all day. All. Day.

Ellen had been waiting for them to return, knowing her boat was the only way back to the island. She sounded the horn on the ferry just for the pleasure of watching her brother jump and risk an avalanche of Christmas presents. Even in the low light, she could discern the evil look he sent toward the wheelhouse. Her grandmother was unfazed and waved to Ellen. The old gal had stamina and spunk.

Switching off the lights in the wheel house to prevent flying insects from being attracted to a good time, Ellen watched the rest of the passengers dribble onto the ferry. This late at night, only overnight guests and returning locals were interested in crossing the dark waters to White Pine Island. Although the bars were an attraction, during the weeknights the ferry schedule was not accommodating to late night bar hoppers.

She rubbed her eyes and was glad this was the last run of a very long day. Snuggling into her sheets was a very appealing thought. If only there were someone waiting for her on the dock, or on her couch, or in her bedroom. Ellen tried to remember if she had always felt lonely on the late night run.

She hadn't. Opening her heart to Pete had also meant opening herself up to loneliness when he wasn't there. She'd felt the same thing when Alex left, but this was different. There was no letdown. No anger. Just an aching wish that things were different.

Ellen glanced at the digital clock glowing over the control panel. There were five minutes left before they had to shove off, but she doubted any more passengers would show up. She picked up the microphone to ask her deck hand to signal her the all clear, and she stopped with her finger on the button.

A man stood below on the deck, his features clearly visible in the glowing Christmas lights. He was alone. Looking up at her wheelhouse. Even without the holiday lights illuminating him, she would know Pete McCormack anywhere.

Ellen's cell phone buzzed and she saw a picture of Pete at the wheel of a golf cart, smiling in the island sunshine.

"Loneliest boat captain on the Atlantic," Ellen said. It was the truth, a recently discovered one.

She heard Pete chuckle. Kept her eyes on him, even though he probably could only see her shadow. She didn't want to look away for fear he'd disappear. And she knew now that she could never let him go.

"I can help with that," he said. "Permission to enter your wheelhouse?"

"Only if you hurry."

She watched Pete shove his phone in his jacket pocket and run across the deck toward her stairs. She lost sight of him for only a moment until he reappeared in her doorway.

"It's been the worst three days of my life," Ellen said. Pete was one of the few people in the world she could be completely honest with. He was her best friend, even if things had to change. She wanted to rush to him and wrap him in her arms. "No matter what you choose to do about moving and getting a new job—"

She paused, a lump in her throat making words difficult even though she knew what she wanted to say.

Pete kept both hands on the doorframe, his eyes on her, waiting.

"I have to have you in my life," she said. "I love you and I can't let you go."

A smile lit his face and he released his grip on the doorframe. They both took a step and were locked together in an instant. This, Ellen thought, was right. Even though she was picking him up on the mainland, he still smelled like Dial soap and pine trees as if he'd never left the island.

But was he leaving?

"I love you, too, Els," he whispered, his lips in her hair. "And these three days have actually been the craziest three days of my life."

Ellen waited, afraid to ask. Pete kissed her on the lips and pulled back so she could see his face. "You know that job interview you flew me to?"

She nodded.

"It wasn't exactly an interview. Oceanview Electric is expanding and they're looking for a partner. They were especially interested in a partner on the island because of all the growth and building going on there."

Hope flapped its wings in Ellen's chest, but she still couldn't speak.

"With my business experience and electrical knowledge, they were interested in adding me to their partnership and making me part owner."

Pete touched Ellen's face lightly with his fingertips and traced the outline of her lips. "I can't believe you're letting me do all the talking," he said.

"I don't know what to say," she admitted.

"What are you hoping?" he asked.

"I'm hoping you'll say you can be their partner and still live on the island."

He smiled. "Not exactly. I turned down their offer."

"What? Why would you do that? It's everything you wanted."

"Not quite everything. I turned down the partnership, but I took a job with them instead so I'd have a steadier income."

"I don't understand," Ellen said. Her emotions were in full fight or flight mode.

"Have you heard there was an offer on my parents' golf cart business?"

She nodded. "But no one seems to know who it is."

Realization dawned on her a moment before Pete said it.

"In order to get the bank to loan me the money to buy it outright from my parents, it helped to have a steady reportable income in addition to the proven revenues from the business."

"It's you," Ellen breathed out. She kissed him and held tight to him, overcome with joy that he would be staying on the island. His lips responded to hers, making up for the past three lonely days.

"Wait," he said, his breath coming quickly. "I still have two problems."

Ellen put a hand on her chest, trying to quell her racing heart.

"With the business to run and a full-time job doing electrical work on the island, I'm going to be pretty busy. I've hired a manager to help me with the golf cart business, but there was one other condition of my employment with Oceanview Electric."

Ellen waited, afraid to ask.

"I have to prove I have reliable transportation, even on short notice, in case they need me sometimes on the mainland."

Ellen laughed, her heart feeling as if it could fly out of her chest.

"I told them I had my own private pilot," he said, rubbing his nose against hers.

"Am I your own?"

"If you'll have me," he said.

"You're everything I want."

She lost her train of thought as she kissed Pete in the ferry wheelhouse. Until someone cleared his throat in the doorway.

"Excuse me," Ned said, "but Grandma is wondering if this ferry is ever leaving the dock."

Ellen glanced over Pete's shoulder and saw her brother, smiling, on the top step.

"You know how demanding she can be," he said.

Ellen reached up and pulled the rope to sound the horn.

"Back to the island," Pete said. "Where we belong."

Epilogue

On Christmas Day, Ellen and her family gathered in a small parlor near the main dining room after a large breakfast was served to their guests at the Grand Hotel. They exchanged gifts and talked about all their plans for the New Year. Her brother Easton got a new cello case. Ned added to his already impressive collection of golf clubs. Kate and her daughter got matching dresses for the New Year's Eve party.

And Ellen's parents got her a set of her very own china. The first dishes she'd ever had that were not recycled from the hotel kitchen.

"Getting domesticated?" Easton asked with a grin. Everyone knew she and Pete were together and the news about him buying the golf cart rental had spread like the wind over the island.

"I think they're beautiful," Bethany said. She was curled up on the floral couch next to Ned, and Ellen had never seen her brother so happy.

Her eyes on the door, Ellen waited for Pete to stop by after his family's gift exchange. She had a special gift for him—a set of electrician's tools in an easily portable and lightweight case for his trips on the ferry or the plane.

She knew the moment he arrived, sensing his presence before she glanced up to see him standing in the doorway of the parlor. He held a large square box wrapped in red paper. Ellen caught her mother's eye and smiled as she joined Pete in the hallway. She grabbed her gift for Pete on her way out.

"Nice outside," he commented. "Want to open this on the porch?"

They sat side by side in white rocking chairs, their gifts on the table between them.

"You first," Ellen said.

Pete tore the giftwrap off his present and admired the tools and toolcase. "Perfect for commutes," he said. He rolled his eyes dramatically. "You know how the airlines can be, but this box looks like it will hold up."

Ellen laughed, happiness rushing over her like ocean waves. "My turn."

She unwrapped the gift and found a photo collage frame inside.

"Take it out of the box," Pete said.

Ellen slid the frame out of the box and discovered there were eight different attached photo frames, each of them with a picture of her and Pete. A kindergarten picture, a photo of them on the swings on the playground in elementary school, eighth grade graduation, a Christmas picture from the island party when they were in tenth grade, a high school graduation picture of them together in matching gowns, a snapshot of them with both their sets of parents at the island's 4th of July fireworks, and a picture of them on the beach with their arms wrapped around each other in the sunshine.

But the last frame was empty. Ellen looked up and found Pete staring at her.

"Did you forget this one," she said, her finger on the empty frame.

He shook his head and took her hand. "I haven't forgotten anything. Not one single moment of our life together so far. That empty slot is for our wedding picture."

Ellen swallowed, smiled, fought tears. "Is that a proposal?"

"It certainly is. I've loved you for twenty years. Marry me, Els?"

"I thought you'd never ask."

They stood, embraced, and kissed. Pete pulled a ring box from his pocket and was poised to flip it open when they heard footsteps behind them. Ellen's entire family—grandparents, her aunt and uncle, her parents, siblings, and cousins stood in a semi-circle on the porch of the Grand Hotel. Ellen's mother, aunt, sister, and cousins Samantha and Cora were teary-eyed, but her grandmother stepped forward and held up both hands.

"Get on with it," she said. "We've got celebrating to do."

Pete dropped to a knee and held out the box. He raised both brows and looked up at Ellen.

"Yes!" she said as she held out her left hand and her family erupted in cheers and applause.

~The End~

A Note from the Author

Thank you for reading Ellen and Pete's story from *Christmas at the Grand Hotel*. I hope you loved it! Please look for the next three books in the series throughout 2017. *Springtime at the Grand Hotel, Summer at the Grand Hotel*, and *Autumn at the Grand Hotel*.

If you enjoyed my work, please visit me at www.amiedenman.com to learn about my other novels.

The Gull Motel
Will Work for Love
Blue Bottle Beach
Under the Boardwalk
Carousel Nights
Meet Me on the Midway
Her Lucky Catch
Her Lucky Prize
A Heartwarming Holiday

I would love to hear from you or connect with you on social media. Please follow me on twitter @amiedenman or find me on facebook.

Thanks, readers! Merry Christmas!
Amie Denman